Hood to Hood 2:

Spank's Revenge

D. M. Gaines

New Flavor
Books

Hood to Hood 2: Spank's Revenge

Visit our website: Newflavorsbooksandpublishingllc.com

New Flavor Books & Publishing LLC
P.O. Box 603323
Cleveland, Ohio 44103

This book is dedicated to everyone from the hood that made it out against all odds. You are the ones that let it be known that anything is possible, no matter the situations or the conditions that you may be faced with. May others follow in your footsteps.

Books by D. M. Gaines

Hood to Hood: A Cleveland Story
Hood to Hood 2: Spank's Revenge
Sexual Addiction: Director's Cut
All Flavors: A Book of Erotic Short Stories
Bisexual Bliss
Hitting' Licks
Murder or Justice
Deadly Surgeon

I would like to give thanks to my son and daughter in law, Kevin and Beverly Johnson. Thanks for all of your help and support. I would like to give thanks to my mother Carol Gaines and her boyfriend Tyrone, thanks for all the ripping and running that you two have done for me. I would like to give a special thanks to my new editor and partner Earvin Taze Watters Jr., Last but not least, thanks to all of you that has purchased any of my books and has enjoyed them.
Sincerely Donaze M. Gaines

Chapter 1

Spank and Kris were in Liberty City sitting in Spank's Navigator. "So when are you going to get back with me?" asked Kris.

"I'm supposed to meet Hosea tomorrow, so I should be hollering at you by the afternoon."

"It's dry and we been losing hell of money. Them Carol City niggas have been up here serving."

"Don't worry tomorrow that all comes to an end." Kris climbed out of the truck and Spank pulled off. He was on his way home to count the money that he had just gotten from Kris. He was supposed to meet with Hosea the next day to get ten keys. Spank had come a long way. When he first moved to Miami a year before, he only had twenty grand to his name. He moved to Miami after being forced out of the game and his hood by his right hand man Tink.

He left Cleveland, Ohio and moved down to Miami for two reasons. To be with a stripper named Cherry, that he met on his first visit to Miami, and to plot his revenge on Tink and the hood that had turned its back on him.

His goal was to get his money up. He rented a place in Liberty City, and started hanging in the Pork and Beans projects. He set out to meet people and develop relationships. The first person that he met was Kris, who was half Jamaican. Kris had been in Miami for seven years. He was fresh out of prison, and was looking to come back up in the dope game, but he had no money nor a connect.

He and Spank developed a relationship, and he introduced Spank to a couple of hungry cats from Pork and Beans that wanted to come up. Spank promised them that they would come up together.

Cherry's roommate was a Dominican name Angelica, whose boy-friend was deep in the dope game. His name was Hosea, and she introduced Spank to him. Spank told him about his crew and his vision, Hosea agreed to sell him one key for $14,000 and see where it went from there. Now here it was a year later, and Spank was buying ten keys of dope.

When he got home Cherry was in the kitchen cooking.

"Hey baby, are you hungry?"

"Yeah, I can go for something to eat, just let me go upstairs and handle something right quick." Once spank came up he bought a house out in South Beach, and Cherry moved in with him. She stopped stripping and focused on school. Spank started paying her tuition.

She called upstairs, "Spank I forgot to tell you that Hosea said call him." Spank came halfway back down the stairs.

"What did you say?"

"Hosea called and asked me to tell you to call him, when you got in." Spank went back up the stairs and called Hosea and he answered, "Hello my friend."

"What's the word Hosea? Is everything a go?"

"Tomorrow morning be at the Saw Grass Mall at ten o'clock."

"I will be there." Spank said then hung up. He was happy that they were about to be back on. Hosea had been out of the states for over a month, and they had run out of work. Niggas from other cities had been trying to move in on them. He was going to make sure that it came to an end. He counted the money and put it into a Gucci bag then went downstairs to eat.

☐

Ten o'clock the next day Spank was sitting in the mall's parking lot. He wasn't there no longer than two minutes before a gold Lexus pulled in next to him. Spank grabbed the bag off of the seat and got out of his Navigator. He walked around to the passenger's side of the Lexus and got in.

"How have you been Poppi?" Hosea asked him.

"I'm doing a lot better, now that you are back. The streets have been dry and we have been losing money."

"Well your worries are over Poppi. I have a new pipeline and I will be lowering the prices for you. From now on you will only pay $12,000 a key. Is that good, no?"

"That's great Hosea. Thanks my nigga."

"You are a good dude Spank. I want to see you prosper. Start doing something with your money, something legit."

"I hear you Poppi. Let me get out of here before the traffic gets thick."

"Okay, call me when you are ready my friend."

"Alright!" Spank said and climbed up out of the car. He jumped in his truck and headed home. When he got there he put five keys into his floor safe, then he called Kris.

"Get everybody together and y'all meet me at the spot in one hour."

"We will be there rude boy."

When Spank arrived at the stash house, Kris was there with Nu-Nu, J-Bo, Jamaican Earn and Rocky.

"What's up?" he greeted them when he entered the house.

"Respect man." said Earn.

"I got a brick for each of you. We are back on, so don't worry about nothing. We ain't ever running out again."

"I say let's celebrate tonight, by going to the King of Diamonds, then we start going hard tomorrow rude boy." said Kris.

"Y'all go ahead, wifey will kill me. I will get with y'all tomorrow." Spank told them.

"Okay, we will see you tomorrow rude boy." Spank left the stash house and headed back home. He was going to chill with Cherry that evening. He went home and they had a candlelight dinner, then went upstairs and had wild passionate sex. Afterwards, Cherry fell asleep, while Spank laid awake. He could not sleep, his thoughts were on Cleveland. He missed his hometown and his hood. His money was up and he had a team. He was thinking that maybe it was time to go back and get what was taken from him.

The next day he met up with Kris and the rest of the crew, and shot his pitch.

"I got some unfinished business back in my hometown. I think now is the time for me to go back and set things straight, I can't do it by myself, so I want to know if y'all are willing to ride with me?" They all felt loyal to Spank. He had kept his promise and put them all on. They felt that now his problems were theirs also.

"We are with you rude boy." said Jamaican Earn. That was music to his ears. He got with Hosea to discuss ways to get his dope shipped to Cleveland.

He explained to Cherry that he had to go back home for a while. She begged him not to go, but he told her it was something that had to be done. He told her that if he wasn't back soon that he would send for her.

The following week Spank, Kris and the rest of the crew took off in two separate cars, headed towards Cleveland, Ohio. While driving Spank thought to his self, "It's time we meet up again Tink."

Chapter 2

"Tink hurry up, we are going to be late!" Coco said. Today was the day of the grand opening for Coco's new hair salon. It was the third shop that she had opened in a year. This one being on Cleveland's west side. All of her salons were named after her slain friend Linda. This was going to be the best salon yet. It had a spa and a massage parlor in it. All of her friends were supposed to attend. It was starting at two o'clock. It was a quarter to one, and they were running late.

Once again she called out to Tink, "Boy, will you come on?" Tink came running down the stairs, while adjusting his suit coat.

"Damn girl, we got time. You won't even let a nigga take care of his business. I had to make sure that Allen had everything set for tomorrow." he said to her, even though it was a lie. He was really checking to make sure that Allen had gotten the surprise that he had in store for her later on.

"This is a big day for me, I just want to get there early to make sure that everything is set up right."

"All the money we paid those contractors and caterers, shit better be right. Come on lets go?" Tink said as he headed for the door. They climbed into Tink's 745 BMW and headed to the west side. They arrived at the shop at 1:30PM. The contractors were done and the caterers had everything set up. Coco was pleased that everything was done just right.

"I told you baby that everything was going to be alright." Tink told her. Coco went to Tink and he gave her a hug and a kiss on her forehead. They heard the bell over the door ring as someone came through the door. They looked up and seen Silvia entering.

"Hey girl!" Coco said to her as they embraced.

"Girl I'm so proud of you, you have come a long way."

"I'm just glad that God has blessed me with a good man."

"I know that's right, I need to find me a good man. I'm tired of Rodney's no good, lazy ass. He is starting to be a heavy load."

"Cut his ass loose girl, haven't you read Steve Harvey's Act like a woman, but think like a man? Men think about themselves, so that's what you got to start doing."

The doorbell chimed again and kept chiming as people continuously filed in. All the women that came in gave Coco hugs, while all the men shook hands with Tink. People tried out the services and enjoyed the refreshments.

Allen finally entered the shop. Tink seen him and waved him over. Allen walked to the back where Tink was at.

"You got it dawg?" Tink asked him.

"Man you know that I never let you down." He reached inside of his jacket and pulled out a black box. He handed the box to Tink, who took it and opened it up and looked at what was inside. He smiled and said, "That's what I'm talking about dawg!"

"Go do your thing baby boy!" Allen told him. Tink went and grabbed his self a drink, then walked to the middle of the room.

"Excuse me everybody." Everyone turned and gave their attention to Tink.

"I have an announcement that I would like to make. Coco could you step over here for a minute please?" Coco walked towards Tink wondering what he was up to. When she reached him, he took her hand into his then turned to face their audience.

"I would just like to say a few words. First I would like to thank all of you for coming out to show your support. This is a special moment, and I'm just glad that we can share it with all of you. Most of you know that me and Coco have been together since our high school years. Well, tonight I'm ready to make it official."

Tink turned to Coco and dropped down to one knee. Coco could not believe what was going on. Her heart started beating fast and tears started to stream down her cheeks as she watched Tink pull out a black box. He opened it, pulled out a ring, then looked Coco in her eyes and asked, "Will you marry me?" Coco wiped the tears from her eyes and said, "Yes!" The shop erupted in applause. Tink slid the ring on Coco's finger then stood up. He kissed Coco then said, "Bring out the champagne!" Allen rolled a cart out from the back that was loaded with buckets of champagne.

Tink passed bottles out and people started popping corks. All the ladies huddled around Coco trying to see the size of the rock that Tink had put on her finger. All the fellas including Big Dame from the Valley congratulated Tink.

Coco had been waiting on this moment for a long time. Tink felt that he no longer had a reason to keep putting it off. They had everything going for them. Now he felt that it was time to settle down and start a family. Dame whispered into Tink's ear, "The shipment arrives tomorrow at three. I'm about to head home. I will see you at the docks tomorrow."

"I will be there, we are about to close shop and head home ourselves." They shook hands, and then Dame left.

By five o'clock Coco and Tink had cleared everyone out of the shop, with the promise that the following day it would be open for regular business hours. They then headed home to continue the celebration inside of their bedroom. They sexed each other into the middle of the night, and then fell asleep in each other's arms.

□

The next day at two o'clock Allen texted Tink and told him that he was outside. Tink grabbed his glock 40 and went outside and jumped into the car with Allen. They headed downtown to the boat docks. The Good Time III was a luxury cruise ship that took people on a cruise from Cleveland to Canada. It made stops in Pennsylvania and New York. Dame and Tink had two women take the cruise, and at the New York layover they were to pick up a package. The package was to contain ten bricks of cocaine. When Allen and Tink pulled up at the docks, Big Dame and his right hand man Flip were already there. They all got out of their cars and walked to meet up with each other.

Dame pulled some binoculars out and looked through them out towards the water. "Right on time!" he said as he passed the binoculars to Tink. Tink took them and looked through them. Off in the distance, he could see a large ship headed their way. "About another thirty minutes and they should be docking." Dame said.

"Man, the city is dry, ain't nothing but B12 and soda around. We are about to serve the whole city." Tink told Dame.

"Be easy, a lot of people got fucked over during the drought. Niggas are going to be real grimy, trying to get back, so watch it."

"Yeah, I feel you."

"Tink, remember all money ain't good money." That's why Tink liked Dame, he was always level headed and insightful.

The ship pulled in and people started to exit the ship. Rita and Tonya came off of the boat each carrying large knock off Coach Purses on their shoulders. Each purse held five bricks. The girls seen Dame and Tink and headed their way. Allen and Tink climbed into the car with Dame and Flip. The girls went and got into the car that Allen had driven in. The keys were already in the ignition. Tonya started the car and pulled off with Dame and Tink following behind them.

"Now that's a sweet route!" Dame said.

"Yeah I like that move!" replied Tink.

"That is why the world is better with democracies, dictators are too closed minded and causes their people to lose out on a lot of opportunities. Since you took over Tink, your people and my people have prospered. Now that is what life is all about."

"I feel you my nigga. I learned a lot from Spank. He was just to bull headed. The team needed new leadership."

"That's the way the world evolves, is through new leadership. Look at Iraq, Libya and North Korea. They are now dealing with consumers that they had never dealt with before and that is going to expand their economies."

"And we are going to expand ours!" said Tink.

Chapter 3

Spank and his crew were on the outskirts of Cleveland. They were on I-71 coming through Brook Park. Jamaican Earn was taking in the sites. "Rude boy, me see that y'all have a lot of things going on up here."

"People are sleeping on us Earn. They think that Ohio has nothing. Columbus has Ohio State, Canton has the football hall of fame and here in Cleveland we got the Rock and Roll Hall of fame. We got the Cleveland clinic, which has one of the most prestige cardiac units in the world. We may be small, but we do our thing, plus we get money."

"What about the city, the ghetto and the clubs rude boy?" asked Earn.

"Everything that Miami has got we have."

"The girls," Spank laughed and said, "Any kind you want." Jamaican Earn pulled out a blunt and lit it. He sat back and smoked. The scent was so strong that Spank had to roll the windows halfway down.

Spank crossed over to 90 East, heading out to Euclid to his house.

Kris was driving the car behind Spank. Nu-Nu and J-Bo were also in the car with Kris. They were glad that they were finally there. They had traveled all the way from Miami with a car full of drugs and guns. Spank got off of the freeway on E. 185th. They drove three blocks, and then turned onto a side street. At the third house on the right hand side of the street, Spank pulled into a driveway. He pulled all the way into the back so that Kris could pull in behind him. Spank, Earn and Rocky hopped out of their car. Kris, Nu-Nu and J-Bo did the same. Spank opened the back door to the house and they started taking their stuff inside. Kris, Nu-Nu and J-Bo unloaded the drugs and the guns. After they took everything inside, they headed back out to the cars. Spank led them to Severance Mall. They parked and headed into a Nextel store. Spank bought everyone phones with blue tooth and texting capabilities.

They stepped outside and Spank called Spud. She answered, "Hello?"

"What's up ma?"

"Who the hell is this?"

"Oh, you forgot me that easily?"

"Is this Spank?"

"Yeah this me."

"Oh my God, where have you been?"

"I was out of town for a minute. I'm back now and I'm trying to see you. I brought some of my dudes down with me, so call a couple of your friends, so that we can have us a little get together."

"Oh okay, what time are y'all coming?"

"I'm about to make a couple stops, then we will be on our way."

"We will be here."

"That's what's up!" Spank told her then hung up,

Their next stop was the state liquor store. Spank went inside and bought a couple bottles of Remy and a bottle of Hennessey. After leaving there Spank headed to Dailey's. He knew how much Earn and Kris enjoyed Jamaican food, so he decided to take them to Dailey's. He wanted to show them that they did not have to miss out on their choice of food, while they were in Cleveland.

Dailey's was family owned and most of the Jamaicans in Cleveland ate there. Spank pulled up and he and Earn got out of the car. He motioned for Kris to join them, and then they entered Dailey's. The smell of curried goat filled their nostrils.

"All rude boy, you know what me like mon!" said Earn.

"Yeah mon me starving!" said Kris. They stepped up to the counter, where Kris ordered oxtails and dumplings. Earn ordered sawfish and

Ackee. Jamaican Mark walked out of a back room and noticed Kris and Earn. Recognizing that they were Jamaican he approached them, "Respect soldiers."

"Respect mon!" Earn returned the greeting. Mark was 24 years old. He was deep in the dope game. He was selling everything from weed, ecstasy and cocaine, he even sold Viagra pills. He talked to Earn and Kris while they waited on their orders. They learned that Mark had only been in the states for two years. Through his menacing ways and shoot first methods, he had quickly risen up in the game in Cleveland slinging weight. He gave Kris and Earn his number and told them to call him if they needed anything. Their orders were ready, they grabbed them got back in their cars and Spank led them down to Spud's house.

Chapter 4

"These niggas got me fucked up!" Rick was telling Byron.

"What they think I can't get at them cause of this chair?" Rick asked Byron.

"I don't know, but they have set up shop by Gene's corner store."

"Well, we are about to close their shop!" Rick said as he was putting bullets into the clip of his Tech 22.

Some niggas from Buckeye had decided to set up shop across from Morris Black, which put them in direct competition with Rick. A year earlier Rick had gotten shot in a robbery that went bad, and was left paralyzed. It took Rick almost a year to come up enough to place workers on the block to pump for him. At first people did not take Rick seriously, do to him being paralyzed from the waist down. He had to lay a few people down for everybody to see that he meant business. Once he got up to a bird he started putting young niggas on the block to pump for him. Byron was one of his workers.

For the past week money had been coming in slow. When Rick questioned Byron about it, he informed him about the Buckeye niggas setting up shop right across the street from where they pumped. Rick felt that even though he did not have any feelings in his toes, that he still refused to let anybody step on them. His motto after getting shot was shoot first ask questions later. Instead of confronting niggas with his mouth, he decided to confront them with bullets in broad daylight.

Byron had stolen a black Monte Carlo that was parked outside in the parking lot. He wheeled Rick out to the car and helped him into the front seat. He folded up Rick's wheelchair and put it in to the backseat.

Byron got in the driver's side and pulled out a Stanley flathead screwdriver and started the car.

"Go up Mt. Carmel and come back down Woodland." Rick told him. Rick tied a black bandana around his face, and then checked his Tech one more time. He knew that Techs were known to jam, so he wanted to make sure that it was working properly. Doc, Ronald and two more guys off of Buckeye were in Gene's parking lot leaning on a green Bonneville. They had been serving up there all week. As long as paper kept coming as good as it was they had no intentions of leaving.

Their block had gotten hot. The detectives had knocked over eight people in the last month up on Buckeye, so they decided to relocate for a little while. They knew that they were in direct competition with the Morris Black niggas, but to them it was enough money out there for everyone. They passed around a Black and Mild as they waited on customers.

Byron drove down Woodland towards 110th. When they got there, Rick used his arms to pull his self up and looked over at the men in the parking lot.

"Go down to 93rd, turn around and come back up." Rick told Byron. Doing that would put the passenger's side of the car on the same side of the street as the store, giving Rick easy access to his unsuspecting victims. When they got to the light Rick adjusted himself until he was in the perfect position.

"Don't let me fall out of this mother fucker!" he said to Byron. When the light turned green, Byron pulled off slowly. Rick had his upper body leaning out of the window. He had the Tech 22 in both hands. As soon as they got within distance Rick started letting off shots.

"Oh shit!' Doc said as he got hit in the shoulder. He fell to the ground and tried to pull his self under the car. Ronald jumped through the car window and laid down on the back seat. The other two guys took off running only to get cut down. Rick swung his arms in a sweeping motion, going right to left, hitting the boys in the back, the buttocks and the back of their legs. He got so hype shooting at them that he almost fell out of the car. Byron had to grab him by the back of his pants to prevent him from falling out of the car.

Byron snatched Rick back inside of the car and sped off. He drove two blocks, over to where Rick had his van parked. He took Rick's wheelchair out of the backseat, helped Rick get out of the car and back into it, then jumped back into the Monte Carlo. He was going to take it down to the reservoir and burn it.

Rick pulled his self up into his van, reached out and folded the wheel chair, and pulled it into the van. He took off heading to his girl Cynthia's house.

Chapter 5

Spank pulled to the curb in front of a house off of E. 81st and Kinsman. It was two streets over from the Garden Valley housing project. They exited the cars and headed up the front steps of the house. Spank knocked on the door and Spud opened it. She had a huge smile on her face as she opened the screen door to let them in.

"They all walked into the house, Spud had her girls Nanky, Robin, Monique and Clarrisa. The girl's eyes lit up when the men filed in. Three of them had gold fronts and two of them had dreads that hung down to their backs. Spank felt someone staring at him. He turned and saw Nanky looking at him with her face all screwed up. "Why the mean look baby girl? You ain't still mad are you?" Nanky just rolled her eyes at Spank. Spud took notice, "She told me that you tried to holla at her Mr. Big Spender."

"Oh, she told you that? Well I'm going to let her have that one. Right now I need to talk to you in private."

"Okay let's go into my room." They headed into Spud's room and she closed the door.

"So what's up?"

"The nigga Tink did me dirty last year. He thought he took me out of the game for good, but I'm back stronger than ever with a stronger team. I am about to reclaim what is mine and I need you on my team. I need you to be my eyes and ears. I do not want anybody knowing that I am back until I am ready to make my move, is you with me?"

"You know you did me dirty Spank and now…" Spank cut her off, "Hold up baby girl, I ain't trying to stay stuck in the past. You tried to play me and I played you instead. There were no victims. I'm on some new shit and I'm trying to cut you in on some real paper. So dead that old shit and let's get this paper you feel me?"

"So what do I got to do?"

"First I need all the information you got on Tink. What he is doing and who he is doing it with. Also I need to use your spot as my command post, until I can get another spot down this way."

"You want to turn my house into a dope house?"

"Never that I am pushing weight I just need to have a stationary spot for me and my soldiers to put our moves together. So what's up with Tink?"

"Him and that nigga Dame done hooked up. They got shit on lock. Tink bought Coco three hair salons. Allen is riding around in Benz trucks and a GT Bentley."

"They are doing it like that huh?"

"Yeah they are doing the damn thing."

"What about Disco? What is that nigga up to?"

"He jumped on a basketball tour. That nigga trying to get money the legit way."

"What has the dope game been like lately?"

"It has been a drought for a minute, but I heard that Dame and Tink just got back on."

"Listen I need you to spread the word that you know somebody that got A1 work and is selling it at a cheaper price than what they are paying. Tell them that you can hook them up with free samples. My man Jamaican Kris is going to be my front man. You are going to bring everybody to him."

"That is a lot of shit that you want me to do for you. What is you going to do for me?"

"I'm going to pay you in two ways, here!" he said throwing her a knot of cash.

"And what is the other way that you are going to pay me?" she asked.

"With this!" Spank unzipped his pants and pulled his dick out. Spud just looked at his dick and her mouth started to salivate.

"You got just what a girl needs!" Spud told him and started taking off her clothes. Spank followed her lead. He stripped naked, then asked her, "How do you want it?"

"I want to taste it first, let me suck it."

"Like Burger King have it your way!" Spank said as he walked towards Spud with his dick pointing straight out. Spud dropped to her knees and took him into her mouth. Spank loved the way that Spud gave head. He thought that she sucked dick like it was an art to it. He said to his self, "This bitch graduated with honors, on a four year scholarship from the school of dick sucking." Spud was looking up staring him in the eyes as she devoured his dick. Spank thought to his self, "I'm going to bust in this hoe's mouth if she don't stop."

He forced Spud off of his dick. He stood her up then picked her up. He carried her over to the dresser and sat her down on it. He then took her left leg and put it up onto his shoulder. Spud put her arms down and used her hands to grip the front of the dresser for support. Spank grabbed his dick and guided it to her entrance. He pushed in and Spud used her arms to push her ass up off of the dresser.

Spank started fucking her, going all the way in then pulling all the way out until only the tip of his dick was still inside of her. Spud was looking down watching his dick go in and out of her. The sight turned her on and she came instantly. Thick white cum coated Spank's dick. He put his hands under her ass and pulled her off of the dresser. She wrapped her arms around his neck and wrapped her legs around his waist, as he stood up in the middle of the floor fucking her. Spud started licking and nibbling on his ear.

"You missed this dick didn't you?"

"Yes! Yes!"

"You want this dick don't you?"

"Oh, Spank damn."

"Do you want it?"

"Yes, give it to me."

"We are going to get this money ain't we?"

"Yes baby! Yes!" The words were music to his ears. Hearing them words made him bust off inside of Spud. He put her down, and when he let her go her legs gave out on her and she fell to the floor. She laid there on the floor looking up at him thinking to herself, "This nigga is the truth." Her body involuntarily shook again. Right then she knew that she would do anything for that nigga.

Her and Spank got dressed, and headed back out to the living room. Robin was hugged up with J-Bo, Clarrisa was sitting on Nu-Nu's lap and Monique was out on the porch with Rocky. Nanky, Earn and Kris were nowhere to be seen.

"Where is Earn and Kris?" Spank asked them.

"They went down the hall with old girl." Spank went down the hallway. It was only one other room down there, besides Spud's bedroom. The door to that room was open and there wasn't anybody in it. He was about to walk back up the hall when he heard some noise coming from behind another door. He walked over and opened the door. He could not believe his eyes. Jamaican Earn was sitting on the toilet with his pants and underwear down around his ankles. Nanky was squatting over him, facing away from him. She was riding Earn as he sat on the toilet and was giving Kris head at the same time, Kris looked up, "Respect mon, Spank she is possessed, fire burns inside her, very wicked mon!" Spank looked at Earn, who just smiled and winked at him.

"Hurry up y'all, we got to get going." Spank told them then shut the bathroom door back. He walked back out front, and all eyes were on him.

"Pay me no mind!" he told them as he indicated for Spud to follow him outside.

"I need to know where that nigga Dame's stash spot is at. Put your girls on him or something, but I need that info like yesterday. I will be back down here tomorrow with some work, so put the word out."

"I got faith in you baby girl, don't let me down." After the way that he had fucked Spud, she felt like super woman and she would use all her powers to do what he needed her to do.

"I got you!"

"One more thing, where that hoe Coco's salons at, and which one does she be at the most?"

"She got one in the Longwood plaza, it's one on Lee road, then they just opened up another one a couple of days ago that's on Lorain Ave. Since that one just opened, she probably be there the most, all of them are named Linda's."

"She named her shit after that trifling bitch?"

"That was her girl, I guess."

"Alright, just handle that shit for me." Spank said as he stepped back into the house. Earn and Kris was coming up the hallway, with Nanky following behind them.

"Us have to come back rude boy, she vexed us" Kris said smiling.

"Don't worry we will be spending a lot of time down here. We got to roll right now though."

They all headed out to the cars and got in. Spank drove down to Longwood. He pulled into a parking lot, cut his engine off and just sat there observing the activities.

Chapter 6

Fred was in the Grafton Correctional Institution. He was sitting outside on a bench with two of his partners Red, and Marquis. He was telling them what he had just found out over the phone.

"They shot my nigga Doc in the shoulder. They hit up Booda and Greg too, Booda made it, but Greg didn't."

"What was it about?" Red asked.

"Don't nobody really know. They were down by Morris Black serving, so they think that it could have been some of them niggas out of the Black set tripping."

"That's fucked up dawg, Greg was a good nigga."

"They say the good die young." Marquis said.

"If I was out there that shit wouldn't have happened." Fred said.

"Nigga who is you, the bulletproof man or something. Your ass would probably be laying up in the hospital right along with them niggas."

"Nigga pass that black!" Fred told him as he took a sip of the foxy.

Later that night Fred was lying in his bunk thinking. He had been locked up for over a year and only had nine months left, as long as he did not lose his good time. He felt it was time for him to get his plans together. This was his fourth time in jail and he was going back out there to nothing. His girl Shannon had vowed to stick by his side, but ended up pregnant by another nigga after he had only been locked up for three months. He knew that he was getting too old to keep doing bits. He figured that this was going to be his last chance to come up.

He still did not have a trade or a skill, and the only realistic thing that he could see himself doing was selling dope. He was relying on Doc and Ronald to be on, so that they could put him on. He had been trying to meet a connect since he had got locked up. There were a couple of big time dope boys there with him at Grafton. One in particular named Keith Hart had half of Cleveland on lock at one time. Fred had been trying to figure out a way to cut into him. They were from two different sides of town. Keith was from St. Clair which was across town from Buckeye.

Fred started to notice that every day at lunch time Keith would be outside under the shack working out. Fred started sliding out there working out. One day he saw Keith working out by his self. He was benching and looked like he needed a spotter. Fred rushed over there to the bench and spotted him, as he benched 315 for ten reps. After he completed the set Keith got up and said, "Good looking, where are you from man?"

"I'm off of Buckeye."

"Oh yeah, y'all be getting money over there?"

"It's mad money, but ain't no constant supply over there."

"You be moving that work though huh?"

"Like a U-Haul truck moves furniture."

"What's your name dawg?"

"Fred,"

"I'm Keith,"

From that point on Fred and Keith were inseparable. They found out that they were getting out a month a part from each other. They made plans to do business together. Fred couldn't wait to be released.

Chapter 7

Allen was down in Longwood sitting in a rental. He was down to one bird left. He had it bagged up in quarters. It was only five o'clock, he still had three more sales lined up. He figured that he would be through before the night was over. Then Tink and Dame could re-up. Unbeknownst to him, two cars had been sitting in the parking lot, with its occupants watching him. They witnessed him make four transactions. Two more cars pulled into the parking lot and conducted business with Allen before he decided to call it a night. He pulled out of the lot and headed towards the freeway, with the cars following him. He got off the freeway in Maple Hts. He drove up to Libby road, and then made a right when he came to Beachwood drive. Down in the middle of the block he pulled into the driveway of a single family home. The two cars pulled to the curb and sat. They watched Allen enter the house and lights started to flick on.

Spank turned to Earn, "I took that nigga under my wing, when he ain't have shit, he was a bum." As Spank talked his voice went up as he got angry thinking about how Allen had turned on him.

"Yeah he living now and that's where he lay his head and keep his dope at. He must ain't never listened to Biggie's ten crack commandments, don't keep no dope where you rest your head at. I guess we can tell them to him, when we relieve him of all the dope and money he got stashed in there"

"Him have no respect rude boy. Bombaclot, we kill him!" Earn said.

"That's my nigga!" Spank said then pulled off.

Later that night Tink and Coco were in bed.

"Hey bae!"

"What's up momma?"

"I got some good news."

"Oh, yeah, what is it?"

"I'm pregnant," Tink sat up in bed.

"Are you sure?"

"Yeah, I took a home pregnancy test, and then I went to the clinic and double checked. I'm six weeks pregnant." Tink beamed with pride. He was finally about to be a father. He reached over and pulled her gown up over her head. He got between her legs and slid up in her. Instead of making love he was fucking her.

"Damn boo, you already got me knocked up. Why are you doing it so damn hard?"

"You know they say pregnant pussy is the best pussy."

"This pussy is so good I might be able to shoot another one up in you."

"You are going to knock this baby out of me, if you keep pounding me like that!" Tink tried his best to calm down. He was just so excited. He pounded her until he nutted then rolled over onto his back. Coco turned to him, "I ain't trying to spoil the moment, but now that we are financially straight, about to get married and have a baby, can you leave the drug game alone?"

"Coco, don't start that again!"

"You said last year before Spank left that you were going to get out. You done took his place and got use to that power and now you don't want to let it go. What are you looking for? It can't be money. We got businesses. What are you seeking Tink? When does it stop? When you get caught or killed?"

"You are tripping Coco, I got people that depend on me. I help people feed their families."

"That's bullshit Tink and you know it, turn the shit over to Allen. He can handle it, you are just addicted to the power."

"You are tripping, I ain't got time for this shit!" Tink said as he got out of bed and started putting his clothes back on.

"Oh, so you are going to leave now!"

"Every time I bring up you getting out of the game, you run!"

"I'm tired of you pressing me, I'm going out for a few drinks, I will be back when I get my head right."

"Keep walking out! One day you are going to come back and I am going to be gone." Tink did not reply he just walked out of the room.

Coco curled up with her pillow and cried. She just couldn't understand why Tink couldn't let go of the game. They had enough money and investments for them to live comfortable for the rest of their lives. She figured that if he got out now that he could be a success story. She felt that if he stayed in the game, that the outcome would be either jail or death. She thought, "Why can't people in the drug game realize where it leads to until they are already there. Should l really have this baby, knowing that he is never going to give up the game?" She laid there and cried herself to sleep.

Chapter 8

A week had passed, and Spank had turned Spud's house into his base of operations. Spud had been doing her job of lining up customers. Kris was the front man. Everybody that Spud introduced to him thought that he had come straight from Jamaica. They had even moved in on Dame and Tink's clientele.

Dame and Tink were waiting on the girls to go and pick up another order for them, they were dry. Word started to travel fast about the Jamaican with the good dope at a cheap price. By the time Dame and Tink had gotten back on, most of their customers were dealing with Kris.

Dame and Tink were sitting up in Lancer's having dinner and a conversation.

"So how has shit been moving for you?" Dame asked Tink.

"Shit has been moving slow. The word is that a Jamaican is up here with A-1 dope at prices cheaper than ours."

"That shit is putting a dent in our pockets too. They must got a straight pipeline, if they are selling their shit with no cut on it."

"Shit! At the prices that we are paying for our shit, if we lower the prices we are not going to make shit!"

"Do you have a solution to our problem?" Dame asked Tink.

"First we got to find out who this cat is, and what he is about. He ain't just pop up on the scene and started serving everybody. Somebody had to help him make connections. We got to find out what is really going on before we can figure out how to handle it. We lay low for about a week, if shit don't pick back up by then, we might have to result to drastic measures, have some shooters on deck."

"You know that beefing brings heat, which causes money to stop flowing."

"Dame is money flowing your way right now? You want to just fall back and let them knock us out the box. I say, we hit them up, and after the heat cools off, we resume normal operations, what is your choice?"

"You know that I am with you Tink, whatever you decide I'm with it."

"Just sit tight my nigga. I am about to put my ear to the streets and see what's really going on."

☐

Spank and his crew sat in two cars outside of the house where they had watched Allen go into the week before. Spank, Earn, Nu-Nu and Kris were in the first car. Spank was talking, "Phase one has put a dent in their pockets. Now it is time for phase two. Soon as he pulls up we are going to force him into the house and make him show us to the dope and money." They got out of the car and signaled for the others to join them.

"Rocky, J-Bo you two stay in the cars, in the driver's seat and stay alert. Everybody else take your positions." Spank and Earn went to the back of the house. Kris and Nu-Nu went up on the front porch and ducked down. They laid and waited for Allen to pull up. They started to get restless as they waited for over an hour. Finally after an hour and a half of waiting Allen pulled into the driveway.

Kris signaled to Nu-Nu to pull his mask down. They crept off of the front porch, pulling out their guns. Spank and Earn already had their mask on with their guns drawn. When Allen stuck his key into the lock and turned it, they rushed him simultaneously. Both pair rushed up on him with their guns drawn. Before Allen had a chance to react, he had four pistols pointed at his face. He did not show any sign of fear, so one of the men slapped him in the head with his pistol. Allen slumped over but was caught before he could hit the ground. They drug him inside the house and shut the door. They took him into his living room and tied him up, then threw him down into a chair, "Where the dope and money at Bombaclot, pussy mon where it at?" Allen would not talk, so again he slapped him with the pistol. This time it drew blood. A river of blood rolled down from the top of his head.

"Tear the place up, split up!" The men split up and started searching the house. One of the men called for everybody to come upstairs. They all rushed to where he was at. He was standing in the master bedroom holding a green duffle bag in his hand. Inside of the bag was seven kilos of coke.

"There is a safe in the closet!" Kris said. Spank ran over to the closet and seen a portable safe. He told Earn and Nu-Nu to grab it. He headed back downstairs. He had some business to handle. He went into the kitchen and turned on the stove then he walked over and opened up a drawer and pulled out a cutting knife. He walked back over to the stove and held the blade of the knife over it until it turned a bright reddish, orange color. He headed back into the living room, and walked over to Allen. He reached out and ripped his shirt off of him. Allen saw that the knife was the color of a branding iron and his eyes got as big as a saucer. Spank laid the knife on Allen's chest. The hot metal seared his flesh. The smell of burned flesh filled the room. The only person that was left inside of the house with him was Kris who looked on in horror. Spank pulled the knife away from Allen's chest with burning flesh still stuck to it. Allen was only semi-conscience when Spank put the knife to the side of his face and whispered into his ear, "Never bite the hand that feeds you." Then he decided to throw a twist into the game, "Dame told me to kill you, but I am going to let you live, so remember that you owe me."

Spank and Kris left the house. Kris turned to Spank, "Enough respect mon, you crazy Booyaka you fry him like goat, bomboclat crazy."
They got in the cars and pulled off. Spank thought to his self phase two
complete.

Chapter 9

A year had past and Man thought that it was cool to return home. He had got hot in Chicago. He ended up killing a man out there and the police were onto him. He was known under an alias out there so he figured that if he bounced he could never be tied to the body. It was ironic that he would leave Cleveland because of three bodies, go to Chicago catch another one then return to Cleveland where he was still wanted in connection with the three. To top it off he went right back up to Morris Black.

He was staying at a girl name Mable's house. Mable smoked premos, wet and popped ecstasy. As long as Man fed her habit everything was cool. To do that Man had to do what he did best, rob people. He didn't have sense to pull robberies in places other than Morris Black. He would go out every night on a late night creep. He would catch dope boys on their late night hustle and stick them up.

He may have been gone for over a year, but the people up in the Black still knew who he was. Word quickly spread that Man was back in town and sticking people up. Word got to Jerrell and Tez. They were on the phone one night talking, "You know our problem is back?" said Jerrell.

"Yeah, I heard that shit is crazy."

"They say he is on that same dumb shit. Ain't no telling when they are going to snatch his ass up."

"Look I know he is blood, but I ain't trying to let nobody take me down forever Tez."

"I feel you aunt Janice will have a fit if she found out that we did him dirty."

"That's why I say weigh out the consequences. Don't anything add up worse than doing life in prison or ending up on death row."

"Damn dawg, I am going to feel fucked up, but I guess we got to do what we got to do. Are we going to tell Ray-Ray?"

"No, the less people that knows the better. We got to stop that trickledown effect."

"Starting tomorrow night, we are going down to the Black and post up like we are dope boys and let him come to us."

"Hit me up tomorrow cuz, I will be ready."

"Bet!" Jerrell said then hung up.

Rick was up in his stash house talking to Byron and his other workers.

"It's been two weeks y'all, we handled that little situation, but money is still coming in slow, what the fuck is going on?"

"Shit! First you got these two homicide detectives Jenkins and Howard. They were sweating the block hard in the daytime. They have been parking in Gene's parking lot, sitting there for hours watching both sides of the streets. They even were snapping pictures and shit. Then at night niggas got to watch it. That nigga Man is back and is robbing anybody that he can catch slipping. He is even robbing the fiends, so they are scared to come through at night." Byron told him.

"His bitch ass is back huh? It's that nigga's fault that I'm in this wheelchair. That nigga left me when shit got thick, he ain't a killer for real. How the fuck do he got niggas shook? I ain't got no legs, but my heart is bigger than most of these niggas around here. What was that old phrase, if you want something done right you have to do it yourself. I'm going deal with them detectives and Man's bitch ass."

☐

Cynthia walked into the room, with a short teddy on that left her fat ass cheeks hanging out. Byron, Mookie and Larry's mouths dropped open. Cynthia was a bad bitch, and she didn't have any shame in her game. They could not understand what she saw in Rick. He was paralyzed from the waist down. They wondered if that meant that, his dick did not work.

Rick saw how they were looking at Cynthia. He knew that everybody was wondering how he had knocked off such a bad bitch. He felt it was because of his gangsta. The bitches recognized his swag and his dick still filled them up.

He decided to high cap on the little niggas, "Cynt baby girl, show these niggas how gangsters get it." Cynthia smiled, walked over to Rick and dropped down to her knees.

She pulled his dick out of his sweat pants and started sucking it in front of the three youngsters. They couldn't believe it. This bad bitch was sucking a nigga in a wheelchair dick in front of them. The crazy part was the fact that Rick was still carrying on the conversation, "See you don't have to have legs to be a gangster. Being a gangster is embedded in your heart, not your legs, y'all little niggas got legs but no heart. Y'all go out and steal a hottie then come back and swoop me. I am going to give them detectives some work in another area, then I will handle Man's bitch ass."

They sat there staring at Cynthia giving Rick head, "Fuck y'all waiting on, go get the car. When y'all show me y'all got heart, then y'all can get some of her throat." They all got up and left.

They headed up to the Buckeye plaza to steal a car. They came upon a Chevy Cavalier. Byron pulled out his trusted Stanley screwdriver. He had Mookie and Larry looking out as he dipped between the Cavalier and the car parked next to it. He popped the door lock with the screw-driver. He opened the car door and remained in a kneeling position. He leaned inside of the car and placed the screw driver in the slit of the column. He popped the plastic off of the column, then broke the horseshoe. He used the screw driver to pull the pin up and the car roared to life. He then climbed into the car and broke the blinker box. He stuck the screw driver inside and broke the pin unlocking the steering wheel. He hit the door lock button opening all the doors. He blew the horn and Larry ran to the car and hopped in. They pulled off driving back to the Black.

Chapter 10

Kim stopped by Allen's house on her way to work that morning. As soon as she opened the door a foul smell hit her. It smelled like shit and urine. She wondered what the hell it could be. Allen's car was in the driveway, so she knew that he was home. She sat her keys on the kitchen counter and walked into the living room. She saw Allen sitting tied up in a chair. His eyes were closed and his chin was on his chest. She ran over to him, "Allen! Allen! Oh my God!" When she got to him she heard labored breathing.

"Thank God! Hold on baby!" she said to him as she ran for the phone. She called 911 and told them that she needed emergency assistance. She gave them the address and they told her that an ambulance was on the way. She hung up the phone, then ran into the kitchen and grabbed a knife. She ran back into the living room and cut the rope off of Allen. When she pulled the piece of cloth that they had stuffed in his mouth out, his phone began to ring on his hip. Kim pulled the phone off of his hip and answered it, "Hello!" Tink was surprised that a girl that was crying answered Allen's phone, "Who is this?"

"It's Kim."

"Why are you crying Kim? Where is Al?" in between sobs she told him, "Somebody burned him, somebody tied him up and burned him!"

"Kim, slow down, tell me what happened?"

"I just stopped by on my way to work and found him tied up and slumped over in a chair in the living room."

"How is he?"

"Pretty bad, I am waiting on the paramedics to get here."

"Okay, listen to me, check the house to make sure that ain't anything lying around that could get him in trouble. The police are probably going to search the house, so make sure that there are not any drugs or guns lying around okay? And keep his phone with you, my number should be on the screen. Call it back when you get to the hospital, so you can let me know which one y'all are at. I am going to come up there."

"Okay, let me go and check the house before they get here." She hung up the phone and told Allen, "Baby hold on, they are on the way." Then she ran around the house making sure that there wasn't anything illegal lying around. Kim thought to herself that her parents would kill her, if they found out what was going on. Kim was not a street girl. She had lived a sheltered life. She was raised in Bedford Heights, She had went to college and got a degree in accounting. She was now working for a major accounting firm.

Her parents had warned her against messing with Allen. It is something about a parent's intuition. For some reason they always know when a person is not right for their child. The first time that she took Allen around her parents, her father had pulled her aside and told her that he was no good. Her mother had called her the next day and told her Allen had given her bad vibes.

Kim could not see any of what her parents were seeing. Yeah he sold drugs, but he treated her good. She had never seen a violent side of him. Until he showed her different, she vowed to herself that she was going to stick by him.

The ambulance arrived and the paramedics put Allen on a stretcher and loaded him into the ambulance. Kim climbed into the back of the ambulance with them. While they were on their way to the hospital she called up to her job. She told them that she had a family emergency and would be late.

They got to the hospital, where they rushed Allen into surgery. He had first degree burns to his face and chest. The seared flesh had to be removed. They also had to remove skin from the back of his calves to give him skin grafts to his face. After the surgery was completed he was transferred to the hospital's burn unit.

Tink had arrived and was downstairs in the waiting area with Kim. The doctors told them that he was expected to make a full recovery, but that because of the severity of his burns, he was going to be in extreme pain. He explained to them that they were going to have to keep him heavily sedated for the next couple of days. He advised them that they would be able to see him, but because of the heavy sedation that he was going to be unresponsive.

Kim debated about staying, but felt that she needed to get to work. Tink needed to find out what was going on. Allen had seven birds that belonged to him. He turned to Kim, "I need to go to the house with you. Somebody robbed him or either tried to rob him. He had something very important that belonged to me. I also know that he had some things that were important to him, so we need to go find out what's up."

Kim got into the car with Tink and they drove to the house. They both searched the house from top to bottom and found nothing. No safe, no dope, Tink knew that they had gotten robbed.

Coco's words echoed in his head. A lot of death had been around him, was he to be next. Allen was laid up fighting for his life and was going to be scarred for life. Was it really worth it. He had to figure that out.

Chapter 11

Later that night Rick was in the front passenger's seat of the Cavalier. Byron was driving, with Mookie and Larry in the backseat. Rick spoke, "It's time for you little niggas to put in some real work. Mookie, when I start firing you start firing, you got me?"

"Yeah I got you!" Mookie said nervously.

"I ain't going to keep doing all the work by myself, so you little niggas can flip on me. Y'all got to get blood on your hands too, or I'm going to have to put you niggas to sleep. I ain't doing life in prison in no damn wheelchair, because one of you niggas flipped. We are all getting dirty tonight.

Byron headed up to E 120th in Buckeye to that Wendy's where niggas be serving at.

"It's time we feed them bullets."

Byron thought, "This disabled crazy mother fucker. How did I get myself mixed up with him?" When they arrived it was a group of guys in Wendy's parking lot, on their late night hustle. "I want you to pull into the parking lot. I want to be close up on them niggas." Rick said.

Byron pulled the Cavalier into the parking lot. The group of guys thinking that they were fiends, started to approach the car, "I got them boulders," the first guy that reached the car said.

"Let me fire them up then." Rick said as he stuck the same Tech 22 that he had caught the other dudes with out of the window and started shooting. Six bullets tore into the first boy's chest. "They are shooting!" another boy yelled as he turned to flee the other way. Mookie had yet to fire a shot.

"Shoot something nigga!" Rick yelled at him. Mookie wildly shot out of the window hitting nothing. There was one last boy close enough to hit. Rick turned the Tech on him and let loose, cutting the boys legs from up under him. He turned to Mookie, "Go finish him nigga or you are dead!" Mookie sat there in the backseat with tears running down his face. The car was silent, all of a sudden Larry said, "Fuck it! I will do it!" He snatched the gun out of Mookie's hand then jumped out of the car. He ran over to the boy that was lying on the ground shaking and crying. "Help! Help!" the boy said when he heard footsteps approaching. He looked up and seen Larry approaching with a gun in his hand.

"Please don't kill me, please!" Larry silenced him with two shots to his face. He took off and ran back to the car and jumped in. Byron zoomed out of the parking lot.

"That should give those detectives something else to do!" Rick said. He turned back to face Larry, "You're my type of nigga. Y'all got to cut this bitch ass nigga Mookie loose, before he bring y'all down. I don't even know if I should let this nigga live. He might rat us out." Sniffling Mookie said, "I ain't going to say nothing!"

"I don't think you will either." Rick said, then turned around and shot Mookie in the face. Byron lost control of the car for a minute and almost crashed. He could not believe what Rick had just done. Mookie's body fell over on Larry. Larry pushed Mookie up off of him.

"Turn down that side street." Rick instructed Byron. Byron turned down the side street.

"Pull over!" he pulled over to the curb. Rick reached his arm into the back and opened up the back door.

"Put him out!" Rick told Larry.

Larry had no intentions of touching Mookie again. He took both of his feet and used them to push the body out of the car, Byron peeled off again. Him and Larry dropped Rick off then went and burned the car. They were driving, when Byron turned to Larry, "Why did you take the gun and shoot ole boy?"

"Because I ain't stupid, I ain't want to get killed."

"Did you see how he shot Mookie at point blank range?"

"How the fuck could I not see it. He did it right in front of my face. That nigga is crazy and we are going to have to play him close. We might have to body that paraplegic psycho mother fucker."

"If we do that, we might as well get everything that he got."

"That's what's up, let's just keep rocking him to sleep. Let him keep thinking that we are lames and when we catch him right we are going to peel his cap like an Idaho potato."

They burned the car and headed back to Rick's place to get the head from Cynthia that Rick had promised them. True to his word Rick had Cynthia suck both of them off. When they left Byron said, "Let's take that bitch too, when we take everything else. They both laughed at that suggestion.

Chapter 12

Kris, Earn and the rest of the crew had become familiar with Cleveland. They had started hanging out in the projects and going to the clubs. They all had in house pussy with Spud's girls, but they found that the girls in Cleveland were live and that they were fond of out of town niggas. With long dreads and gold fronts they stood out. Niggas knew that they weren't from Cleveland. They even had a different style of dress. Niggas did not like the fact that they were from out of town, getting money in their city and fucking their bitches.

One night they were all at the strip club called the GP. They had a table in front of the stage and they were buying out the bar. A group of dudes off of 93rd and Union were sitting at a table behind them talking.

"Who the fuck these niggas think they are. Y'all are going to let them niggas come up in here and high cap in our hood?"

"Randy, chill the fuck out. Them niggas ain't bothering nobody!" Rudy told him.

"Man fuck that, they throwing money around like they are the shit."

"Hey Shabba Ranks, why y'all don't take your asses back to Jamaica!" Randy yelled at Kris and his crew.

Kris and Earn looked at each other, "Him rude boy, no respect mon!" Kris said. They turned and looked behind them at Randy's table.

"Yeah we are talking to you two, Shaggy and Super Cat looking mother fuckers." Kris, Earn, Nu-Nu, J-BO and Rocky all stood up and approached the table behind them. The guys with Randy stood up. It was only two of them, Leon and Will.

Leon spoke, "Pay our friend no mind, he is just drunk."

"Shit, I ain't drunk. Fuck these goat eating mother fuckers."

"Bomboclat, me cut your tongue out bony."

"You won't do shit to me!" Randy said and lunged at Kris. In a flash, Kris whipped out a Swiss knife and cut Randy across his throat. When Randy's two friends tried to rush to their friend's aide they were viciously beat and stomped by the rest of Kris' crew.

The bouncers were finally able to get things under control. They forced Kris and his crew out of the club. They tried to tend to Randy, who was lying on the floor clutching his throat. He was choking on his own blood. Kris had slit his throat from ear to ear.

Kris and the crew started making their presence felt everywhere they went. At the first sign of trouble or disrespect directed their way they reacted swiftly and shrewdly. They knew that you could not get guns into most clubs, so they all kept a knife with them. Quickly they showed people in the city that they were not to be fucked with.

☐

Spank had started staying out to his house more. He wanted to keep his focus on getting even and did not want to chance being seen and blow his plans. He already had phase three thought out in his head. He planned to carry it out the next night.

He started thinking about Cherry. He felt that Spud was alright, but she wasn't Cherry. He missed Cherry, so he decided to call her. There was a two hour time difference and she was already in bed. His call woke her up, she answered, "Hello?"

"Hey sleeping beauty," she instantly woke up.

"Oh, hey baby!"

"Do you miss me?"

"Of course I do."

"Well then, I'm booking you a flight for tomorrow, so that you can come up here."

"You want me to just up and leave."

"At least for a couple of days. I need to see you."

"I can't get ready that fast."

"All you need to bring is yourself. We will buy everything new that you need, when you get up here."

"What about school?"

"We will figure it out. I'm going to die if I do not see you." Cherry felt flattered that he wanted to see her so bad. She wanted to see him also.

"Are you going to have someone pick me up from the airport?"

"I am going to be there to pick you up. After I call and make the arrangements, I am going to call you back and let you know what time your flight will be leaving. And I will know what time it will be arriving here."

"Okay, I guess I will see you tomorrow then."

"I will call you back in a little bit."

"I love you."

"I love you too." Spank said then hung up. Spank called Delta Airlines and booked her a flight that would be due to arrive in Cleveland at six o'clock. Spank figured that would give him enough time to pick her up, take her to get a few things then drop her off at the house. He then could go and complete phase three.

He called her back and told her when her flight was leaving.

Chapter 13

Detectives Howard and Jenkins sat in their car up in Wendy's parking lot.

"What do you think this is all about?" Howard asked Jenkins.

"I don't know it doesn't seem like a robbery. They died with dope and money in their pockets. Then the one they shot in the leg was only to stop him so that they could walk up on him and shoot him at point blank range in the face."

"The coroner said that the bullets that were embedded in his legs were different from the ones that hit him in the face."

"That means that he was shot by two different shooters at different times."

"These were premeditated no doubt, maybe it is a rivalry. It is going to be hard to find a witness that was out that time of night."

"What about the body that was found a couple streets over. What is your take on that?" Jenkins asked Howard.

"His body was dumped there. The way his body was folded up, it looks like he may have been pushed out of a car. You know that they are most likely connected?"

"Why do you say that?"

"The coroner's report says that the two that were shot at this scene, were hit with Tech 22 bullets, and that other fella was also hit with Tech 22 bullets. And now that I think about it, the shooting that happened down by Morris Black, those guys were also hit with Tech 22 bullets."

"You think that all three of them are related?"

"It's a good possibility."

"We got to make sure that all those bullets get over to the crime lab to have ballistics and comparisons done, I will get with the medical examiner."

"Do you have the address for the boy that survived the shooting down by Morris Black?"

"Yeah, he stay two streets over from here."

"Well, let's pay him a visit." Jenkins said as he pulled out of Wendy's parking lot. Howard gave him the address. Within five minutes they pulled up in front of a two family house. They went up to the house and rang the doorbell. A middle-aged, short, black woman answered the door.

"May I help you?"

"Ma'am I am detective Jenkins and this is my partner detective Howard. We are investigating the shooting that involved Donte Fields. We would like to talk to him, do you think that is possible?"

"Sure, come on in." She led them into the living room and told them that they could have a seat. She walked to the top of the steps that led down to the basement and yelled down, "Donte come up here for a minute." Doc came up the stairs.

"What is it ma?"

"It is some people here that would like to speak with you, come on into the living room." Doc instantly became nervous. He knew that it had to be the police. When he walked into the room, there were two detectives sitting on the sofa. They rose, when he entered the room. They noticed that his arm was in a sling. Jenkins spoke, "Donte, I am Detective Jenkins and that is detective Howard. We are investigating the shooting of you and your friend Gregory Smith. We would like to ask you a few questions, please have a seat." Doc took a seat in a recliner chair.

Jenkins started the interview.

"Donte do you know who shot you?"

"No."

"Did you get to see the shooter's face?"

"I couldn't see the person that was driving and the guy that was shooting had a bandana tied around his face."

"Do you remember what type of car they were in?"

"All I know is that it was either black or a dark blue."

"You have no idea why y'all were targets?"

"You sure it was not because you guys were selling dope on someone else's turf?"

"We were not selling dope!"

"Listen Donte, we are not vice, we do not care about no drugs. We only care about violent crimes and homicides."

"Now both of you are from up in this area, but were shot in a parking lot across the street from Morris Black. That is a project that has been beefing with this neighborhood for a while now, so you can't tell me that you guys were just down there chilling in that parking lot."

"I don't care how you put it, we were not selling no dope. We were down there trying to holla at some girls, when a car drove past shooting. I was hit first, Greg tried to run and got hit, that's the end of the story."

"Well, I'm going to leave you with my card. If you can think of anything that could help us solve your friend's murder, you give us a call." Jenkins told him. The detectives got up and headed for the door. Doc's mother escorted them to the door.

"These kids have no respect for truth or authority." Howard said.

"Yeah, but what can you do? Let's head down to the station and see what we can find out about those bullets."

Chapter 14

Tink was up at the hospital visiting Allen. Allen was sitting up and he was going through a lot of pain. Every four hours he was given a shot of morphine.

"How are you doing?"

"I'm living but I feel dead. Did they get the shit?"

"Yeah, they got the dope and your safe too."

"Shit! They caught me slipping Tink. It was four of them and they got the drop on me. That safe contained all the money that I had to my name, but I promise you that I am going to pay you back, if I have to work it off."

"That's the furthest thing from my mind right now. I want to see you get healthy and I want to get the niggas that did this to you. Did you see their faces?"

"No, they all had on masks. It's crazy though, I was half conscience when one of them whispered in my ear saying that Dame wanted him to kill me, but that he was letting me live, so I owed him."

"Are you sure that he said Dame's name?"

"I'm 100% sure! I won't forget what he said or his voice, which eerily sounded almost like Spank's."

"Like Spank's?"

"His voice was similar to Spank's, but deeper."

"What the fuck would Dame have to gain, from taking you out?"

"I don't know, but I would be careful if I was you. I wouldn't trust him until I figured out what is going on."

"Yeah, you're right a lot of fucking shit has been going on lately, and I have no answers for none of it. So when are you supposed to get out of here?"

"They say I got to go through one more operation, another skin graft to my face. So I am looking at another two weeks at least in here."

"You go ahead and get healthy, I'm going to check back with you in a couple of days. I got to get out in these streets and see what the hell is going on, I trusted Dame and if I find out that he had anything to do with this I'm going to lay his fat ass down and that is my word. You be easy little homie." Tink told him then left.

☐

Coco was at her shop, she had a full house including her friends Silvia and Renee. The three of them were in her office. Silvia picked up a book off of her desk.

"Hood to Hood: A Cleveland Story By Donaze Gaines. Girl who is reading this hood book?"

"I am!"

"And why are you reading hood books?"

"To see how they end. This is the only one that I have read so far that has a success story in the end. In most of them, the main character either gets killed or goes to jail."

"I'm having a hard time trying to get Tink to see that."

"You are still tripping with him about getting out of the game?"

"You damn right, I'm pregnant now. I do not want to have to raise a baby by myself. If this nigga ends up dead or in jail, that is what it's going to be."

"That nigga is getting money girl." said Renee.

"How much money do you need? We got enough money to last us for a lifetime. Plus we got plenty investments. Shit, our children will be straight."

"It is hard for them balling ass niggas to give up the game girl. It doesn't even be about the money. It is the rush, the excitement and the status that shit is hard to let go." Silvia said to Coco.

"Well he is going to have to let that shit go or let me go, because I can't do it anymore."

"So, what are you going to do, give him an ultimatum?"

"You damn right, if he loves me and want me to have this baby and be his wife, then he is going to have to let that shit go."

"More power to you girl."

"Y'all, come on let me get out there and make sure that my shop is in order." They all headed back out into the shop.

Chapter 15

Spank picked Cherry up from the airport and took her to the Lakewood mall. He got her a few things to hold her over until he could take her on a full shopping spree the next day. They left the mall and he took her to the house. He explained to her that he had some business to handle that night. He promised her that the next day he was going to take her on a shopping spree and a tour of the city. He told her that they would top it off with dinner.

☐

He left the house and headed down to the stash house. He had rented a house that was right around the corner from Spud's house. The rest of the crew was waiting for him. He got there and they were already dressed and ready. He switched into an all-black outfit, grabbed his mask and they jumped in the cars and headed to the west side. They got off the freeway on W. 117th and Lorain. They drove down to W. 95th. On the right side of the street was Linda's salon and spa.

"Pull around the corner." Spank told Nu-Nu. Rocky was driving the other car. He followed them around the corner. They pulled over. Spank told Nu-Nu to keep the car running. Him, Earn and Kris got out of the car. They walked back to the second car. Spank told J-Bo to come on and told Rocky to keep the car running. He turned to everybody and said, "Word is, there is a wall safe in the office."

"When we go in y'all cover everyone in the front. Don't let anybody in or out. Me and Kris are going to snatch the bitch into the office and

make her open the safe. It is that simple, do y'all got it?" Everybody shook their heads yeah.

They walked around the corner. When they got outside of the salon they each put their mask on. They rushed into the salon with guns drawn, catching everyone off guard. It was close to closing time and there were only two hair dressers, with one client each in their chair. One client was lying back with her hair under a hairdryer. The other one had her head under the faucet in the sink, getting her hair rinsed. The two workers seen the mask men enter. One screamed, and Spank quickly approached her and slapped her with his pistol across her face. He put his finger up to his face indicating for everyone to be quiet.

Earn locked the door and turned the sign around, that said the shop was closed. Coco had been in her office on the phone when they barged in. She heard the yell. Thinking that it was a customer they may have had their scalp burned from lye or hot water she ended her call and went to investigate. She stormed out of her office, only to run into two men with guns that were in mask. She looked past them and seen that there were two other men in masks and holding guns pointed at her workers and their clients.

"Back in the office bitch!" one of the men said to her. Instead of turning her back on the men she backed up into her office. The two men entered and closed the door behind them.

"Open the safe bitch!"

"What safe?" Coco asked trying to play it cool.

"The safe with the money in it bitch. Stop playing games." Coco was trying to figure out, how they knew that Tink had a safe in her shop. She hesitated too long for the men.

"Oh, you think it's a game bitch?" Spank said as he stepped to her and slapped her with the pistol. Coco crumbled to the floor. Spank reached down and started tearing off her dress. She tried to fight back, until he smacked her again with the gun. He snatched her up to her feet and bent her over the desk, and then he ripped her panties off of her. She tried to plead with him.

"Okay I will open it, please don't!"

"It's too late for that bitch!" he told her as he rammed his dick inside of her. Coco screamed out in pain. He put the barrel of the gun to the back of her head and told her that if she didn't shut up, he was going to blow her brains all over the desk. Coco quickly shut up, and cried inside from the pain that she felt from, him pounding her insides out. While fucking her he leaned over her and whispered into her ear, "I should of did this a long time ago. You lucky Tink is my boy." He pulled his dick out of her pussy and slammed it into her asshole. She felt a searing pain shoot through her body as he ripped her asshole apart. Abruptly he pulled his dick out of her because he did not want to leave any DNA inside of her. She crumbled to the floor again.

"Get up bitch, and open the safe before I give my partner a go at you!" Coco struggled to get up off the floor. She stumbled over to the wall and removed a large picture from it. Behind it was a safe mounted inside of the wall. Coco put the combination in and the safe clicked open. She felt something cold running down the insides of her legs. She looked down and seen thick blood running down her legs, "My baby!" she said to herself as she started crying again. She slid down the wall holding her stomach. She crouched there on the floor and cried. Spank stepped over her and emptied the safe, which was packed with neatly stacks of money. He did not know how Spud had happened to come across that information, but to him she was a God send. He and Kris each held a bag as they stepped back out into the salon.

The lights had been dimmed, as if the shop was really closed.

"Let's go y'all!" he said then walked to the door and unlocked it. They all filed out of the shop, pulling their mask off as they got outside. They quickly walked around the corner, jumped into the cars and pulled off. The two workers ran into the shop's office and saw Coco sitting on the floor covered in blood. One of the workers grabbed the phone off of the desk and dialed 911.

The ambulance came and transported Coco to Metro hospital, where later she learned that she had miscarried. They had two give her six stitches in her anus from Spank ripping her apart.

Chapter 16

The next day Spank took Cherry out to Randall Park Mall. They shopped for over three hours, getting everything that she needed. They bought clothes, shoes, perfumes, purses and toiletries. They left the mall and went to the Outback Steakhouse and had a late lunch. After that he took her on a tour of the city. They stopped at Tower City to see the array of stores and Galleries that they had. They went down to the Rock and Roll Hall of Fame. Last he took her down to the flats, on the water, where they sat on a bench and talked.

"So, what have you been up to Spank?"

"Just getting things in order and taking care of business."

"Do you have plans on moving back here?"

"I don't know, why, you don't like it?"

"It is alright, but it is not Miami. No palm trees, no season round good weather, also I do not know what type of job opportunities they have here."

"You do not have to work, I will take care of you."

"Thanks but no thanks, you know that I like being independent. I am in school, because I want to pursue a career."

"Look I haven't written anything in stone. Let's just enjoy these couple of days that you are going to be here."

"Come on let's go." They walked hand in hand back to the car. Spank headed to Long John Silver's so that they could have dinner. They resumed their conversation over dinner. "Spank I know that you came back up here to get some type of revenge. What happens after you get it? Will it stop? Will you feel satisfied?"

"You love getting deep on me, don't you?"

"I just want to see where your head is at and what direction that you are headed in. That way I can know if I want to follow you or not. I want to live a stable and normal life Spank. For a year we have been doing well. We were just fine, but whatever happened up here you just couldn't let it go. I need to know exactly what you are seeking and when will you be at peace."

"My business up here is almost complete. Once I have finished it I will be at peace. All I ask is that you give me time. Let me tie up these loose ends, and then everything will be alright. They finished dinner then headed home. When they got there, they headed straight to the bedroom where they made wild and passionate love. Afterwards they fell asleep in each other's arms.

☐

The next day Spank went down to Spud's house. She opened the door with an attitude. Spank sensed it.

"What is wrong with you?"

"All you are doing is using me Spank, I figured it out, and you haven't changed. You are the same old Spank. All you care about is yourself."

"Where the hell is all this shit coming from? What is wrong with you hoes?"

"Oh, so your other bitches are complaining too huh?"

"Spud stop tripping and tell me what the hell you are talking about?"

"I'm talking about you playing me. I have done everything that you have asked of me. I could be dead if certain people even find out some of the things that I have told you. I done even found out where Dame keeps his stash at, but all you do is treat me like shit. You haven't taken me anywhere. The only time that I see you is when you want some information or a quick fuck. I am worth more than that Spank, way more than that!"

"Spud you tripping, we ain't together, I did not promise you that we would be together. We entered into an agreement and I have kept my end of the bargain. I offered you a proposition and you accepted it, so how do you figure that I am using you? Money and dick is what I offered you and that is what you will keep getting, besides you know why I don't go out. I haven't been out anywhere since I been up here."

"Spud don't go catching feelings and start tripping. If I cannot trust you I won't feel comfortable. Check your emotions and let's keep getting this paper, now give me that info on Dame." She gave him the info, and he fucked her and left her in bed crying.

Spud knew that she shouldn't have fucked with Spank like that. The old feelings that she used to have for him had resurfaced, and had her tripping. She knew that she had to be careful. Spank had given her an indirect threat. She did not want to end up dead. "It's all about the money." she told herself.

"I got to stick to the script and get money.

Chapter 17

Tink was up at the hospital again, this time he was visiting Coco. He had tears in his eyes behind this one, after finding out that she had gotten raped and miscarried the baby. He was ready to kill somebody. He just needed to know who that person was. Somebody was making his life miserable. They were trying to destroy him in every possible way. He thought that it had to be somebody close to him. They had hit Allen for his bricks, now they had cleaned out the safe that he had in Coco's shop. That safe had $250,000 in it. The only thing that he had left was his mind, and he felt like he was losing it.

Coco had been in a shell, she had not said one word to Tink. Every time he tried to touch her, her body would stiffen up on him.

He tried talking to her again, "Look Coco, I need to know who did this to you, so that I can handle it. You got to give me something to go on, did you see their face? Come on just shake your head yes or no." Coco shook her head no. Tink felt some relief, she was starting to communicate with him. "Did they say anything to you?" Coco's body started to shake and she started crying. Tink put his arm around her and she leaned her head on his shoulder.

"He said that he should have done it a long time ago, but that he was your boy."

"He said he should have did what a long time ago Coco?"

"I guess rape me! He was raping me when he said it!" She started crying hysterically.

"He killed my baby! He killed my baby!"

"Shush, it is going to be okay." Tink told her as he kissed her on top of her forehead. He was thinking about what was said to Coco. "I should have done it a long time ago, Tink is my boy." They told Allen, "Dame told me to kill you." Could it really be Dame? Who else could it be? He had to do something soon. If Dame was all he had, then it was Dame that he had to see.

☐

Allen was out of the hospital and he needed to go and see him, so that they could get a plan in effect. Allen was at home still healing from his wounds. He had been burned so deep in his chest that the wound was healing from the inside out. His face had undergone three skin grafts. He realized that his face would never look the same. He would forever have an ugly scar on the left side of his face. He boiled on the inside, he had a thirst for revenge.

Kim had been spending her evenings with him. She did not care that he was broke or that he was permanently scarred. She loved him and showed him through her actions. Allen was thankful for her, she was all that he truly had.

He was ready to get back into the streets and get that paper. Tink had called and told him that he was on his way over to talk to him. Allen was hoping that he was coming to tell him that he had some work for him. The doorbell rang and he went and opened the door. Tink walked in with a gloomy look on his face, "What's wrong fam?" Allen asked him.

"Shit, I don't even know how to say it. Just thinking about it is ripping me apart."

"Let it out dawg, it can't be that bad."

"Some niggas ran up in Coco's shop and robbed and raped her. They killed my seed dawg!" Tink told him as he broke down crying. Coco was pregnant and they caused her to miscarry. I am going to kill them mother fuckers Al. I swear that I am!" Allen dropped down in his chair and put his head down. He thought to his self, "This shit is getting crazier by the minute.

"I'm sorry to hear that dawg that is some foul shit. We got to find these niggas and kill them. Whatever you need me to do you know that I'm with you."

"She said that the nigga told her that he should have done it a long time ago, and that I was his boy. It's all pointing to Dame even though there is a voice in the back of my head telling me that it ain't him. I got to pay that nigga a visit Al!"

"It's your call homie, I'm down with whatever you decide to do!"

"Tomorrow we are going to pay him a little visit."

"For sure, just come through and swoop me when you are ready."

"Shit we might as well try to get him for everything that he got. We both are fucked up, if it don't make dollars then it don't make sense, so let's get it all!"

"I feel you homie, just come get me."

☐

The next night Tink, Allen, Pee-Wee and Ricardo went to Dame's house out in Richmond Heights. They were taking a chance going way out there instead of waiting to catch him in the city. There weren't that many blacks out there and the police still engaged in racial profiling in Richmond Heights. Tink felt that he had to make it known to Dame that he could touch him anywhere. Tink knew that if he was making the wrong move that he was forever going to destroy him and Dame's relationship, but at that point he did not care, he was on the edge. He felt that somebody knew something and he needed answers.

They pulled into Dame's driveway. The only one that had their face covered was Allen. They all got out of the car and approached the front door with pistols in their hands. Tink rang the doorbell, and a voice said, "Who is it?"

"It's Tink."

"Oh! Hey Tink," Tasha was saying as she opened the door. When she had the door halfway opened, Tink kicked it with his foot. The force of the kick caused the door to slam into Tasha's face breaking her nose. They all rushed into the house, Tink dragged Dame's baby mother by her hair over to the couch and threw her onto it. Ricardo covered Tasha with his pistol, while Tink and Allen ran up the stairs.

Pee-Wee heard a noise coming from the kitchen and rushed in there. There were two kids, a boy about nine years old and a girl about the age of twelve. They looked up in horror when Pee-Wee ran into the kitchen. He told them to keep quiet, get up and come into the living room. He escorted them into the living room and had them take a seat next to their mother.

Tink and Allen got to the top of the steps and followed the noise that was coming from a television. It led them to the master bedroom, Dame was sitting on the bed counting money, when they entered. The scene gave Dame a guilty appearance. Dame looked up and saw Tink and Allen and quickly tried to reach for his gun that was on the night stand.

"Do it and I will splatter your fat ass all over that wall!"

"Tink what the fuck is going on, you running up in my house, where I rest my head with my girl and kids with guns drawn?"

"Pay these guns no mind. Allen would you kindly grab that gun, so that he doesn't try anything stupid." Allen walked over and snatched the gun up off of the nightstand.

Tink resumed talking, "Dame that wouldn't happen to be my money that you're sitting there counting now would it?"

"Tink, what the fuck is you talking about?"

"Somebody ran up in Coco's shop and cleaned out the safe. They raped her and killed my seed."

"Tink I am truly sorry to hear that, but what would make you think that I would have anything to do with something like that. You know that ain't my steeze."

"That's what I thought, but after what happened with Allen."

"What happened with Al?"

"Show him Al." Allen pulled the bandanna from around his face. Dame looked at the scar running down the left side of his face and cringed, "Tink man, I had nothing to do with that I swear that I didn't."

Allen finally spoke, "That's funny, because the nigga that did this to me told me that you wanted him to kill me. He specifically said your name."

"Tink, Al I swear to y'all on my kids man, I ain't have anything to do with nothing that y'all are saying happened to y'all. Not Coco's shop and not what happened to you Allen. Someone is trying to frame me, set me up or something."

"Well until you can prove that's what is going on, I am going to have to relieve you of them ins that you got right there and whatever you got elsewhere in the house. Now you know that your family is here, so let's not play games. Give me the money and we will be up out of here."

"I can't believe that you are doing this Tink!"

"Nigga! My bitch got raped. My seed was killed. You are lucky that I am giving you the benefit of the doubt and am leaving your family intact. Now get your fat ass up and get them ins!" Dame got up off of the bed and walked over to the corner of the room. He bent down and pulled back the rug. There was a floor safe underneath it. Dame turned the tumbler right to left entering the combination. When the safe opened up, Dame backed away from it. Tink walked over and looked down into it. He let out a whistle when he seen all the money that was in it. He instructed Allen to keep his gun turned on Dame while he walked over to the bed. He picked up a pillow and shook it out of the pillow case. He walked back over to the safe and started pulling the money out and putting it into the pillow case.

After Tink emptied the safe, they led Dame downstairs, where his girl and kids sat on the couch. Two men stood, over them holding them at gunpoint. Dame's blood started to boil. They came into his house with guns and scared lil babies. He was going to make them niggas pay. Dame wasn't a killer but he did have niggas willing to put in work for him. They were hitting him for half a meal ticket, but he had been smart enough not to keep all of his eggs in one basket. He had more ins and intended to spend them getting back at Tink and Allen.

Tink led his crew out of the house. They got into the car and pulled off.

"You think you did the right thing letting that nigga live?" Allen asked Tink.

"That nigga ain't no killer, he lucky that I let him live. I don't have any concrete evidence on him, but if I do get some, I'm going back to murk his ass." They went to Allen's house and counted all the money that they had gotten from Dame. It added up to $642,000. "This nigga, had over half a million dollars!" Allen said in disbelief.

"Dame has been in the game for a long time, without doing any bits. That is probably only half of what he's got. He's smart, he wouldn't keep all of his money in one spot."

"So you think that he is still holding?"

"No doubt! That nigga still got doe that's why he is not going to be quick to do anything stupid. I am going to use this money to get some work. After we get rid of all the work, we will split the money up between the four of us. Is that cool?" Everybody said that it was cool.

Tink left Allen's house, went and dropped Pee-Wee and Ricardo off and headed home.

Chapter 18

Man had Mable on the bed fucking her doggy style. He had her facing the dresser and watched his self in the mirror as he was fucking her. She was working her pussy. He liked the way that she gyrated her ass, while backing it up on him, Mable was a beast. If she didn't get high, she would be alright. She had turned Man out on ecstasy. They would both take it then have all night fuck sessions.

One night she got so high and freaky, that she licked his asshole. The feeling was so good to Man that his asshole muscles got loose and he farted. Mable kept right on eating his ass despite the horrible smell. A smell that made Man grab his own nose.

Mable looked back at him, "Put it in my ass!" Man pulled his dick out of her pussy and stuck it in her ass.

"'Yeah that's it, that's how I like it, work that ass nigga." Man fucked her hard in the ass, but it only gave her pleasure. She bucked back on his dick.

"My body is on fire!" She told him as she reached between her legs and grabbed his balls. The warm feeling Man got from her playing with his balls, made him bust off. He unloaded his semen into her ass. After he finished he fell over onto his back. Mable still on her hands and knees told him, "Let me clean you up." then she put his dick into her mouth. Instead of using a wash rag to get the film off of his dick, she used her mouth. She had done that before and actually had tried to kiss him in the mouth afterwards, which disgusted Man. After she finished cleaning his dick with her mouth she rolled over onto her back as well and turned her head towards Man.

"You ain't did nothing all week. You know that I go through mood swings, when I go without. You need to get out there and make something happen!"

"I will go out tomorrow night."

"That is what you said last night Man. My refrigerator is empty, I'm empty. You need to go out there and lay one of them niggas down. You just can't be laying up in here broke, a bitch got needs and bills."

Man was getting tired of her shit. To him, the bitch was like a Hoover vacuum cleaner. She sucked up almost any drug that she could get her hands on and was never satisfied. He figured that it was time for him to find another spot. He got up and started putting, on his clothes. Once he got dressed, he grabbed his pistol, checked to make sure that it was loaded, grabbed his jacket, and then headed out of the door.

Tez and Jerrell were getting fed up. For two weeks they had been looking for Man. They would ride through in the day time and post up like drug dealers at night. They had never once seen a sign of him. They thought that the last lick that he had hit must have been a good one, since he had not been out trying to rob anybody. If he was back in Cleveland he was keeping a very low profile Tez thought. He had not contacted one family member. He must have known what they had planned for him. They stuck to the script faithfully. Tez told Jerrell, "I will never forget what my father told me. He said that patience is a virtue."

Every night they went up to the Black and posted up for a couple of hours. One would stand out in the open, while the other hid. They did this to give the impression of being a sweet lick.

That night Tez was the dope boy. He stood on the block with a black hoodie on. He actually had rocks on him and was serving the fiends. Jerrell stood in the doorway of a building. He also had on a hoodie. In the front pocket of his hoodie he had a 9mm. He was also acting as the lookout for anybody looking suspicious walking up.

About 1:30 in the morning a person came around the corner with a black leather coat on and a pro model hat pulled low down over his eyes. Jerrell came to full attention, pulling his gun out and putting it down at his side. Tez seen the figure approaching too. He turned his back to him while he was approaching and pulled his gun out. Jerrell left the doorway and started creeping up behind the guy. The guy waited until he was all the way up on Tez before he said, "Run that!" Tez turned around and Man seen his face. Man's eyes grew larger than life.

"Tez what's up cuz?"

"What's up cuz?"

"I just been chilling, laying low."

"Nigga you ain't been laying low!" Came a voice from behind him. He turned and there stood Jerrell holding a pistol that was pointed at his chest.

"You should have stayed where you were at Man. We can't chance you being up here and getting caught. Your mouth is too loose, you might give us up."

"Come on we are family, I would never flip on y'all. If y'all want me gone I will leave right now and never come back."

"You had your chance, it is too late now!"

"Come on y'all!" Tez and Jerrell both fired shots hitting him. Once Man fell to the ground, Tez shot him once in the head. The two of them then fled the scene. They felt like a big weight had been lifted off of their shoulders.

Chapter 19

Detectives Jenkins and Howard were up in Morris Black. "If we could get rich off of working homicides, this project alone would make us rich." Jenkins said.

"A lot of killings do go on up here."

"It is like it's convenient, because there are no streets that run through. It is secluded, which makes people feel that it will be easy to get away with it."

"They need to have 24-hour housing authority up here."

"Maybe you need to make that suggestion."

"Maybe I will."

"Let's talk about this victim."

"Okay, what about him?"

"He was shot multiple times by different guns at close range. He died holding a gun in his hand."

"How do two individuals get that close to a person that has a gun in his hand and get the drop on him?"

"Two ways, either it was a set up or he knew them."

"That sounds sensible." Jenkins phone rang, he answered and listened to the caller. After listening, he told the caller thank you and ended the call.

"They just identified the victim and you're not going to believe who it is."

"I'm ready, try me."

"It was Marcus Mills, the guy that we have been looking for, for over a year now."

"The one that we got the tip about?"

"Yeah, that's him, they implicated him in a shooting that happened up here that left one man dead and another paralyzed and the unsolved shooting of the man and woman found murdered last year."

"Do you think that this could be a revenge killing?" Howard asked Jenkins.

"Maybe so, it is almost the anniversary of last year's killings. Come to think of it last year we found ourselves buried in murders. We had the captain and the Mayor breathing down our backs."

"Yeah I remember, maybe it is the weather."

"What do you mean?"

"It seems like every year around this time the murder rate goes up. It is like it heats up and everybody comes out then the trouble starts."

"Well it is back to the drawing board."

"I have found something out." said Howard.

"Oh yeah, what's that?"

"The same gun was used in the Morris Black shootings and the Buckeye shootings. All of the bullets were the same, and the ridges on them were all the same, which indicates that the bullets were fired from the same gun."

"That is a big help, now all we got to do is track down the shooter. I bet you any amount of money that he is somewhere around in this area, Jenkins."

"Well it is time that we do the notification honors."

"That is the worst part of working homicide, notifying the people about the death of a loved one."

"Yeah that gets me too."

"It gots to get done so let's go do it." Jenkins said and pulled off.

Chapter 20

Earn knocked on Spud's door. She opened it wearing only a t-shirt that left her pussy exposed, she had on no panties. She opened the door and just turned and walked away. Earn's dick instantly got hard as he watched her naked ass jiggle as she walked away. He stepped in and closed the door behind him. He tripped off of the fact that Spud did not even try to cover herself up.

He sat down on the couch and Spud went back into her bedroom. A moment later she called out for him to come back into her room. He got up and went back to her bedroom. Spud was sitting on her bed Indian style, polishing her toenails. Her thick, black bush was fully exposed. She said, "You ain't got to be shy, sit down." Earn sat on the end of the bed. He could not believe that he was feeling uncomfortable. He thought that maybe it was the fact that a man that he considered to be his friend, girl was coming on to him.

She was acting like she wanted to give him some pussy, "Spud girl, what ya doing. You Spank's girl, no?"

"Me and Spank ain't got nothing going on. We fuck from time to time that is it."

"Why you do dat?"

"Do what?"

"You know, show your stuff to me, me no botty boy, me beat the pussy up."

"You think you can beat this up?" Spud asked him as she laid back. She used her fingers to spread her pussy lips apart.

"Me pussy killa, mandingo."

"Yeah that's what they all say."

"You wanna know? Me show you anaconda." Earn stood up and unbuckled his pants.

"Wanna see bomboclot, me show you." He dropped his pants to the floor. He did not have any drawers on.

Spud could not believe her eyes. He had the biggest dick that she had ever seen. It hung almost down to his knees and looked like the size of a man's wrist. She then understood why he called it an anaconda. It was uncircumcised causing it to look like a snake.

"Me real Jamaican pussy killa, you wanna play, come now." Earn said while stepping out of his pants. Spud got scared, she really only wanted to get back at Spank. She wanted to try and make him jealous. She did not want to ruin her pussy trying to do that. She thought that fucking one of his friends would make him jealous, but to her it looked as if she had chosen the wrong friend.

"Come girl, come now!" Earn said as he crawled onto the bed. Spud scooted back, until her back was up against the headboard. Earn grabbed her by her ankles and pulled her to him, "No run, me show you me pussy killa baby girl." He got in between her legs and put his dick to her entrance. Being that it was uncircumcised it did not start to hurt until he was half way in, by that time her pussy felt full. To her it felt like she could not stretch anymore.

"Yes baby girl, super tight!" Earn said as he sunk further into her. Spud kept trying to scoot back. He took her legs and bent them back to her chest, putting her in the buck. He placed his full weight on her and sunk all the way in. Spud thought to herself, "He is killing me!" Earn started fucking her.

"Me show you now, you no play with me, no tease me. I am original rude boy, don dodda." He fucked Spud long and hard. She could not believe that she was taking it all in like that. It started feeling good to her. Her pussy adjusted to him and the way that he was fucking her, made her pussy juices flow. The position that he had her in made it hard for her to breath. To her it felt like he was in her chest.

"Let me get on top." she asked him.

"Alright baby girl, wanna ride the horse? Come now." Earn pulled out of her and rolled over onto his back. Spud rolled over on top of him. She got flatfooted and squatted on him. She took her hand and guided his dick to her pussy. She slowly sunk down on it.

"Ride don dodda baby girl!" She placed her hands on his chest and started riding him in a slow rhythm. Her being on top put her in control and lessened the pain that she had been feeling. She started getting into a groove. She dropped down and took him all the way in. She sat on top of him and grinded her pussy on his dick. She even started talking shit back to him.

"Me real rude girl. I throw my pussy like a lasso and pull you in!" She rocked on him until her body shook, and she started cumming. Earn felt her pussy muscles constrict. He rolled her back on to her back and pounded her. Spud took it like a champ, until he finally dumped his load into her. Earn got up off of the bed and said, "You dangerous, you do dat, me pussy killa."

"Yeah you a pussy killa." Spud told him as she took her hand and massaged her pussy. She thought to herself, "His dick game is crushing Spank's." She wanted to sink her claws into Earn after what he had done to her. She knew that he had paper, and she had heard that Jamaicans treat their girls like queens. Her last thought before dozing off was, "Out with the old and in with the new." Earn had put her ass to sleep.

Chapter 21

Jenkins and Howard were at Tone's mother's door. They knocked and she answered the door. She saw the two detectives and thought that they were there to tell her that they had finally apprehended her son's murderer. A tear fell from her eye before she even gave them a chance to speak.

"Ms. Smith if you do not remember I am detective Jenkins and this is my partner detective Howard and we interviewed you last year about your son's murder."

"Have you found him?"

"I'm afraid not. We are still diligently trying to solve the case. Unfortunately as of right now we have no new leads. We are here now concerning another matter. We have you listed as the next of kin for a Marcus Mills."

"Yes, he is my nephew."

"This is difficult to tell you, but he was found shot to death up here in Morris Black two nights ago."

"Oh my Lord!" Tone's mother said as she broke down crying.

"I thought that he was not even in Cleveland, no one has heard a thing from him in over a year. Are you sure that it is him?"

"Yes ma'am, we are sure. He was positively identified through dental records. We need you as his next of kin to come and identify his body."

"I don't think my heart can take it, I am liable to fall dead. My God! What is this world coming to?"

"You will be okay Ms. Smith. I know that you are going through a tremendous amount of grief right now, but before we are able to take any further steps with his body, we need a family member to ID him."

"Let me grab my purse." Tone's mother grabbed her purse and left with the detectives.

While heading down to the morgue Jenkins decided to question her to see if she could provide them with any significant information.

"Ms. Smith did you know that we have been looking for your nephew for over a year now?"

"No, I did not know that. I did know that he had disappeared without a trace."

"We had gotten a tip last year alleging that Marcus was involved with whatever may have happened to your son. Would you happen to know anything about that?" Tone's mother thought for a minute. She concluded that since Man was dead that it did not make any sense to lie.

"Man was there when my baby was killed, he told me what happened." Jenkins and Howard exchanged glances with each other.

"What did he say happened Ms. Smith?" asked Jenkins.

"He said that some boys were trying to rob Rick and when they tried to come to Rick's aide, the guys started shooting."

"Who is Rick Ms. Smith?"

"Some hoodlum that is riding around in a wheelchair now. He got shot, when my baby got killed."

"And you say that this Rick was supposed to be the target of the robbery that went wrong?"

"That is what Man told me."

"And this Rick is now in a wheelchair?"

"Yeah, and I heard that he hasn't changed either. He is still doing the same dumb shit that got my baby killed." Jenkins thought back to when they interviewed Rick while he was in the hospital last year. He had left out the fact that Marcus was there when the shooting took place. He thought that maybe they needed to pay him another visit. He could be involved in Marcus' murder.

They took Tone's mother to ID the body, then dropped her back off at home. They thanked her for her time and the information that she had given them before they left.

Tone's mother went into the house and called Tez, he answered. "Hello?"

"Tez, this is Shirley."

"Oh, hey what's up Auntie Shirley?"

"I need to see you and your cousins. Y'all get over here as soon as possible!"

"Okay auntie, we will be there." They hung up from each other, Tez thinking that something was going on with his auntie called Jerrell and Ray-Ray. He told them that he was on his way to pick them up. He went and picked them up and headed over to their Aunt Shirley's house. When they got there she let them in.

"What's up auntie?" Jerrell asked her.

"The police just dropped me off from identifying Marcus' body. They said that he was killed up here two nights ago. Did y'all know that he was back in Cleveland?" Jerrell and Tez played dumb. Ray-Ray never really knew that Man was back in town.

"No auntie, we had no idea!" They all said in unison.

"That's fucked up!" said Ray-Ray.

"Man crossed a lot of people Auntie Shirley, he should not have come back." Tez said.

"Y'all sure do not act like he was y'all's family. Y'all are just sitting up here all nonchalant, after I just told y'all that your cousin was killed!"

"Shit, we care auntie, what do you want us to do, cry? We see death every day, it's fucked up what happened to him, but what can we do that's life" Tez told her.

"I ain't dumb, I know how y'all get down. Man is y'all blood, do not let his death go without being rectified. That is all that I have to say, y'all can go." They all got up and filed out of her house.

Once in the hallway Ray-Ray asked, "So y'all don't know what happened to him?" Tez could not lie to Ray-Ray. They had done too much dirt together. He just lowered his head. That was all the answer that Ray-Ray needed. They got into the car and rode out.

Chapter 22

Spank had been doing everything that he could to make Cherry happy. She told him that she just did not like the vibe of the city, or the vibe that she was getting from him in his city.

"What do you mean I have changed? I told you that I stay low."

"In your own mind you might think that you stay low as you say. To me you are different, you were more laid back in Miami, you seemed happy. Since you have been up here, you have been nothing but tensed. You have been talking all crazy in your sleep. It is obvious to me that there is something that is bothering you."

"I'm just trying to stay focused that's all. I told you that I am almost finished with what I have to take care of. Just give me a little more time."

"You can have all the time you want, but I am going back home tomorrow, I have to catch up on my schoolwork."

"Are you sure that's all that you have to catch up on?"

"And what do you mean by that?"

"You sure you ain't trying to catch back up to no nigga?"

"Spank you know what, I'm not even going to go there with you. I should be asking you that question. Maybe your unfinished business up here involves a woman. All the late night disappearing, what is all that about?"

"Believe me Cherry, it ain't about a bitch. You seriously believe that I would fly your ass up all the way here, if I had a bitch up here?"

"Honestly I do not know, it's like I don't even know you anymore. This cold calculating side of you I don't like it. I am flying out tomorrow. When you get through with whatever you got going on up here and your ready I will be at home."

Spank just let it go. He decided to take her out for her last night. He took her to the Spy bar, which was in downtown Cleveland. It was an upscale club, with a canopy as well as a red carpet that led from the street to the door of the club. It was multilevel. It had three different floors that played three different types of music. Spank chose the floor that played R&B music. They got a table and Spank ordered them a bottle of Cristal.

They had not spoken since they had left the house. After a couple of drinks, Spank led Cherry out onto the dance floor. They slow danced to Donell Jones' *Where I wanna be*. Spank held Cherry close and tight as they danced. Cherry's body remained stiff. He could tell that she was not really there, and he started to get mad. He thought to his self, "I'm trying to do everything that I can to make her happy. I done jeopardized my shit by coming to a damn club. Fuck it, she wants to go back, she can take her ass back tonight!" He grabbed her hand and pulled her roughly off of the dance floor.

"What is your problem Spank?"

"I'm sick of your damn attitude, far as I'm concerned, you can carry your ass back to Miami tonight. You can catch a late night flight, let's go so that you can pack your shit!" They were maneuvering through the crowd towards the door when someone called out, "Hey Spank!" Spank turned and locked eyes with Silvia. He quickly turned back around, "Shit!" he said as he half drug Cherry out of the club. He even caused her to break one of her heels. He knew that now his cover would be blown. He was trying to figure out what a ghetto ass hoe like Silvia was doing up in the Spy bar.

They got into the car, while driving to the house he called Kris and told him that there was a change of plans. He told him that they had to make that move that night. He told him, "Get everybody together and meet me at the stash spot in one hour." He went home, dropped Cherry off, changed into an all-black outfit, grabbed his gun and headed out of the door. When he got to the stash house everybody was there except Earn.

"Y'all ain't seen Earn?" Spank asked them.

"Him not answer his phone rude boy." Kris told him.

"Fuck it, we got to go. I went to a club tonight against my better judgment. I got spotted, by tomorrow if not tonight people will know that I am back in Cleveland, so we got to run up in the nigga Dame's stash house tonight."

"Now this should be quick and easy. He got the shit stashed in this bitch named Adrian's house. We are going to run up in that bitch's house and terrorize that bitch until she gives us the shit. Nu-Nu you are going to be the driver. We are going to take the van for this one."

They all double checked their guns and ammo then went and hopped into the van. Spank directed Nu-Nu over to E. 96th and Harvard. They turned down a side street, "The green house right there." Spank told them. Nu-Nu pulled to the curb in front of the house.

"J-Bo I want you to stay on point outside of the house, come on y'all." They all got out of the van except for Nu-Nu. They walked up the driveway. J-Bo posted up by the side door. Spank, Kris and Rocky went around to the back of the house. There was a door that led into the kitchen. The door had a square window inside of it. Spank took the butt of his gun and hit the window two hard times cracking the glass. He then used his gloved hand to push the glass in. Pieces of glass hit the floor. They all stood still for a minute to see if anyone would react to the noise from the glass falling. After a minute passed Spank reached his arm inside of the door and unlocked and opened it. They all rushed in.

Rocky remained downstairs, while Spank and Kris headed up the stairs.

There were three bedrooms. The first two were occupied by kids. They came upon the third one, and saw that there was a woman in there asleep under the covers. They went into the room. Spank wanted to show her out the gate that he was serious. He reached out and snatched her up by her hair and slapped her across the face with his pistol. She tried to scream out in pain but Spank covered her mouth. She saw Spank and another man standing behind him with a gun. She started to wonder if her kids were alright.

Spank bent down and whispered in her ear, "You got family, you got kids that can grow up and be somebody. Don't stunt their growth. Dame's fat ass ain't worth you losing your kids, so I'm going to give you one chance and one chance only to tell me where the dope is at. Shake your head if you understand me?" Adrian shook her head indicating that she understood. Spank took his hand away from her mouth.

"In the basement behind the furnace!" She told him.

"Good girl!" Spank indicated for Kris to cover her and headed downstairs to the basement. He got down there and went over to the furnace. He reached behind it and pulled out a black gym bag. He unzipped it and looked inside.

"Bingo!" He headed back up upstairs. He went back into the bedroom and told the girl, "Tell Dame that Tink said now we are even!" He turned to Kris, "Tie her up so that she won't try anything dumb." Kris grabbed a pair of pantyhose that were lying on the floor, and used them to tie her hands behind her back.

They went back downstairs and headed out the door with Rocky following behind them. When they got outside J-Bo fell in line. They all jumped in the van and Nu-Nu pulled off.

"Quick, fast, and easy, just like I told y'all." Spank reached into the bag and pulled out a neatly wrapped brick of cocaine. There were six more inside of the bag. They went to the stash house put the dope up then went their separate ways.

□

Spank did not want to have to deal with Cherry and her attitude. He decided that he did not want to see her until it was time for her to leave. He headed to Spud's house. When he pulled up to her house, he noticed that Earn's rented Dodge Magnum was parked outside. He wondered what was up with that. He parked and got out of the car.

As he walked up to the house he pulled out an extra set of keys that he had to it. He opened the door and entered the house. All of the lights were out. It sounded like a television was on in Spud's bedroom. He headed back there, and opened up the bedroom door. Earn was sitting up naked in Spud's bed with his hands folded behind his head leaned back against the headboard. Spud was naked on her knees, with her face in Earn's lap. Her ass and pussy was facing the door. Spud's head game was so good, that Earn had his eyes closed enjoying the feeling.

Spank's body filled up with rage. He walked over to the end of the bed, brought his leg back then kicked Spud dead in the crack of her ass. His kick caused Spud to bite down on Earn's dick. Earn howled like a wounded wolf. Spud rolled over on the on floor in complete pain. Spank advanced on her and started stomping her into the floor.

"You dirty bitch, this how you do me huh? This how you do a nigga that was good to you?" He stomped her repeatedly in the head, and kicked her viciously in her stomach and pussy.

Earn reached and grabbed his gun that he had stashed under her pillow before they started getting busy. He half stood up, with the pistol in one hand and with his other hand he was covering his dick which was still in pain.

"Rude boy, what cha do dat for? You don't care for girl no? Her come to me, pussy killa."

"Earn this ain't got nothing to do with you, this bitch crossed me. Me and you are supposed to be partners. This bitch is playing games trying to come between us."

"Baby girl choose don dodda. You hit baby girl no more." Spank had left his gun in the car. It was looking to him like Earn was really hung up on the bitch.

"Earn I brought you up here, I put you on, this is how you are going to act towards me about a bitch?"

"Me Jamaican gangsta, me put self on, me put in work, me need no one."

"Okay, if that's how you feel, you are on your own, we are done." Spank turned and headed out of the room and left the house.

Chapter 23

Coco was at her mother's house. She had been staying there ever since she had gotten out of the hospital. Tink had been coming over every day begging her to come back home, but she refused to. She blamed him for the loss of their baby. She felt that his thirst for the game had brought violence to her doorstep. She had gotten brutally raped. She loved Tink, but she just needed time to herself, and she wished that he could understand that.

Her cellphone rang, she looked at the screen and saw that it was Silvia calling and she took the call.

"Hello?"

"Hey girl!" Silvia was hype. She got right to the point.

"You ain't going to believe who I saw out at the club last night?"

"Silvia, I ain't got time for no gossip right now."

"It was Spank!"

"I don't care if it was the man on the moon. I'm not on that shit right now. Call me back when you really got something to talk about!" Coco hung up on her. Just as she hung up the phone, her mother called her and told her that Tink was downstairs. "Shit!" she said to herself, "Why can't I get any peace?" She got up and went downstairs. Tink was sitting on the couch. She let out a deep breathe and sat down.

"What is it Tink?"

"I've come to take you home!"

"I am not ready to go home, I won't feel safe there."

"Coco I will protect you with my life. I am sorry about what happened and I swear to you that I am going to leave the game alone for good. If that is what you want then that is what I'll do. I love you Coco.

We have been together too long. We have stuck together through some of the worst times that we could have ever faced. Let's not change up now."

"I can't take it any more Tink. I have been having a feeling in my gut for a long time that something bad was going to happen. I tried to get you to listen, but you wouldn't, now our baby is gone." Coco started crying and Tink went to her. He sat beside her and put his arm around her to comfort her. Coco laid her head on his shoulder and just let it all out. "I know baby, I know." Tink said comforting her. After Coco got herself together, she sat up.

"I'm serious Tink, I'm just tired."

"I know baby, I'm tired too. Go and get your things and let's go home."

"You promise that you are through?"

"I promise!" Coco went upstairs and got her things and they headed out to Tink's car. Tink started the car and pulled off. When he got to the end of the street he got stopped by a red light. While they were waiting for the light to turn green a gray minivan pulled up along the driver's side of Tink's car. The side door of the van slid opened and a man in a ski mask let off rounds from an automatic assault rifle. The bullets ripped through the driver's side of Tink's car. Tink tried to duck, but the bullets tore through the car door tearing into his side and back. Coco screamed as she was hit with shards of glass. The van sped off. Tink was slumped over.

Tink! Tink!" Coco yelled. Tink was unresponsive. Coco opened her door and stepped out of the car. She bent over and reached back into the car. With both of her hands she grabbed Tink's arms, and with all her strength she pulled his upper body towards the passenger's side of the car. Once she got his upper body over far enough, she closed the passenger door and ran around to the driver's side. She opened the door, bent over into the car and grabbed his legs from under the dashboard and pushed them over to the passenger's side. She jumped into the driver's seat and took off headed for the nearest hospital.

Dame was sitting up in another house that he owned out in Mentor, Ohio. Ever since Tink and his boys had ran up in his house, Dame did not feel safe in Cleveland. He moved his family out to Mentor.

His phone started to vibrate. He looked and saw that he had an incoming text message. The message said, "It's done!" Dame did not know how to feel, he really liked Tink. He just could not understand how things had gotten to the point where they were at. It's only so much that a man can take. Dame was still in doubt about retaliating even after they had violated him in the worst way by invading his home. He had tried to take into consideration everything that had happened to Tink. The robbery of Allen, the robbery and rape of his girl. Then the loss of his unborn child, but after he ran up into Adrian's house, that was the last straw. Dame felt that his hand had been forced. He put a hit out on Tink. The text message had just let him know that the hit had been carried out successfully. Dame felt no pleasure, no peace, no nothing. He just felt numb. He knew that there was still an unseen force out there that was manipulating them. Somebody had turned Tink against him and Dame needed to find out who it was.

Coco stormed into Huron hospital screaming hysterically.

"I need help! Help! he's in the car, come bring him in." Some paramedics with a gurney rushed outside and pulled Tink out of the car. They placed him on the gurney and wheeled him inside. The emergency room doctor cut his shirt off to examine him, while nurses took his vitals and hooked him up to an IV. His pulse was very low and he was losing a lot of blood. They rushed him into surgery. He had flat lined twice, while he was on the operating table. They had to clip and seal a ruptured artery to get him stable enough to finish the surgery. Tink had massive damage done to him. His left kidney was damaged beyond repair. He had a ruptured spleen and his colon was damaged. He was going to have to be permanently fitted for a colostomy bag.

Because of the massive damage Tink lapsed into a coma. The doctor told Coco that it was typical for that to happen when the body had experienced that much damage. He told her that it tends to send the person into shock, which causes them to lapse into a coma. Coco wanted to know how long would he be in the coma. The doctor told her that no one could determine that. He informed her that only Tink's body could make that determination. He told her that truthfully it could take days, weeks or even years for him to come out of the coma, if he came out at all.

The hospital's waiting room was filled to capacity. Allen and almost everybody from Tink's crew were there. Allen was talking to Coco, "Coco tell me exactly what happened?"

"He came and got me from my mother's house to take me home. When we got to the light at the end of my mother's street a van pulled up on the side of us and started shooting."

"This shit is crazy, it can't be nobody but Dame's fat ass. I told Tink that he was making a mistake by letting that nigga live. I got it, you got my word Coco I am going to take care of this one!" Allen took the crew outside.

"Look we are going to split up into groups and search this city for Dame's fat ass. That nigga is to be shot on sight. I don't care if he is spotted in the front pew at a church or on the inside of a police station. I want that son of a bitch dead. Matter of fact, I want anybody that is close to him dead, including that nigga Flip."

They all split up into groups, jumped into their cars and started searching the city looking for any sign of Dame or anyone that was close to him.

Chapter 24

Word of Tink's shooting got back to Spank. With all the things that he had accomplished, he did not feel happy. He thought that revenge was supposed to be sweet. He had been putting all of his energy into getting revenge on Tink, that he was allowing other parts of his life to fall apart. He had been under tremendous stress lately. Him and Cherry's relationship was on the verge of collapsing, Jamaican Earn had jumped camp, he joined up with Jamaican Mark at Dailey's. Earn and Mark started snatching Spank's customers. Giving them even better prices than Spank was. To top it off that snake bitch Spud had sided up with Earn.

Spank did not know if it would be worth the trouble to kill her. He knew that it would bring beef with Earn. Everything that was going on was starting to take a toll on Spank physically, mentally, and emotionally.

Down in Miami he was living, having fun. Since he had been back in Cleveland, he had not experienced any excitement or fun. He felt that he wasn't living life. He thought that maybe it was because he was hiding in his own city. He thought to his self, "Maybe it's time to let it be known that I am back."

☐

Spud was furious about what Spank had done to her, she wanted revenge. She thought to herself, "He has dogged me for the last time." She knew that she could not feel safe as long as he was roaming the streets. She came up with a solution. She decided that she was going to blow his cover. She decided that she was going to let Dame's and Tink's people know that Spank was behind everything that was going on between them. She called her girl Adrian and told her to pass her number on to Dame and to tell him to call her. She told her to tell him that she had some very important information for him. Adrian passed the number on to Big Dame. Dame called Spud, Spud told him that she had information that would make clear who was behind everything that he was going through. She told him that they needed to meet face to face, so that she could explain everything to him. Dame being leery of a setup, after learning that Tink's people were looking for him, told Spud to meet him at Friday's out on Mayfield road. He told her to meet him there at four o'clock.

At four thirty they were both seated inside of a booth in TGIF. Dame asked Spud if she wanted anything and she said no. They got straight to business.

"So what information do you have for me?"

"I know who the person is that has been turning you and Tink against each other."

"You do?" Dame raised an eyebrow.

"And who would this person be?"

"It's Spank!" Dame put a crazed look on his face.

"Spank! How do you know it's Spank?" Spud knew that she could not tell him the whole truth, so she decided to skip around it.

"He came to my house a couple of months ago with a crew of people that he brought from Miami, two of them were Jamaican. He told me that he had come back to get revenge on Tink."

"What does him wanting to get back at Tink have to do with me?"

"I guess he found out that you and Tink had linked up, so he wanted to do things to knock both of you out of the box. He manipulated things behind the scene to turn y'all against each other."

"Things like what Spud?"

"Robberies and shootings."

"And how do you know all of this?"

"Because I eavesdropped on him when he was having conversations with his crew at my house."

"So, let me get this straight, two months ago Spank showed up on your doorstep with a group of niggas from Miami, and he told you that he had come back to get even with Tink?"

"Yeah"

"Let me ask you this, why would you let this shit go on for two months allowing many people to get hurt, and now all of a sudden you decide to come forward?"

"My conscience ain't got nothing to do with what goes on in these streets. Ain't none of them a friend of mines. I just feel that shit has been getting out of hand. After I heard what happened to Coco I figured that Spank was taking things too far. I know that he wants you and Tink both dead. I just decided to give you a heads up. You can take it or leave it."

Dame sat there thinking. It all started to make sense.

The Jamaicans pushing the dope, the robbery of Allen and Coco. It all had been set up to make it look like Dame had been involved. It seemed unbelievable at first thought, but the more that he thought about it the more possible that it seemed. He did not fully trust Spud. He figured that she had to be more involved than what she was letting be known. He also felt that her reason for coming forward had to be different from the one that she had given him. He thought that what was really important was the fact that now he knew who was behind all of his problems. He now knew who needed to be dealt with. He thought that it was unfortunate that he did not find out what was going on before he sent his shooters at Tink. He knew that he could not take back what had been done to Tink, but he knew that maybe that if he could get through to Allen what was really going on, then he might be able to stop the madness.

If he and Allen could join forces he thought that together they could go after the real enemy. "Spud you know that it is an all out war going on right now between my click and Tink's. A lot of blood has been shed. I need you to tell all that you have told me, to Tink's man Allen. Will you be willing to do that for me?"

"I will do it, just do not forget how I am helping you. I am going to need a little compensation for what I am doing." Dame thought to his self, "This shiesty bitch, so her real motivation is money." Dame figured that he needed to play her close.

"Don't worry, I got you. I am going to try to set up a meeting with Allen. Whenever I can get it set up, I am going to get back with you okay?"

"That's cool."

"Look, do you think that you could get me a location on Spank? Can you lead us to him?"

"I think I may be able to do that. It may take a little time, but I think that I can make it happen."

"I am going to give you my cell number. As soon as you come up with something, you get at me alright?"

"Yeah okay." They got up, left out of the restaurant and went their separate ways.

Chapter 25

Larry and Byron were playing their positions. They were pumping dope for Rick. They were bringing in money left and right. They had Rick under the impression that Morris Black was back pumping. Truth be told, the Black was hot as a popped firecracker. After the police had found Man's body, they had been swarming all over Morris Black.

Larry and Byron knew that the only way they could build Rick up, was to make him think that the dope was moving up there. Really they were going to other people's blocks and posting up late at night. When many hustlers would call it a night. Byron and Larry would set up shop on their block. Their plan was to build Rick up to two birds, then stick him for everything that he had before they bodied him.

They were sitting up in the house with Rick while he counted some money.

"You lil niggas have been doing good. Keep this up and y'all are going to graduate up off of the block. I am going to put you niggas on some real weight, can y'all handle that?"

"Hell yeah!" said Byron excitedly.

"We are ready to lock shit down Rick."

"Plus we are ready to get off that hot ass block" Larry told him.

"So you niggas think that you are ready for the big leagues. I'll tell you what, I am going to give y'all a half a bird. I want $14,000 back. It is going to be powder so you can do whatever you want with it. You can water whip it, or use soda. But know this if y'all try to blow the shit up and end up fucking it up, I am still going to be looking to get paid my 14 stacks. So be very careful about what you do. Y'all got a week to get back with me." Byron and Larry felt ecstatic, they were about to be on.

Rick gave them half a brick. They went up to the dollar store and bought a Pyrex cooking bowl, a box of baking soda and a cake mixer. They went back to the Black, put the stuff up, then went on the hunt for cook it up Pete. Pete was one of the best at cooking dope in their neighborhood. He was known for being able to blow dope up, and keeping it good enough to sale. Pete was so good at whipping dope that he could turn four ounces into eight and you could still get them off. He charged ten grams off of every eighth that he blew up.

They found Pete down at the carwash on 93rd. He was washing cars when he could not find any work cooking dope. Since big mouth Marcus had died wasn't any real ballers up in the Black. Pete was washing a car when they entered the carwash. He was soaping the car up when Byron and Larry approached him.

"Cook it up Pete, what's up?" Byron asked.

"What do y'all little niggas want? Y'all are trying to hustle Ole Pete on the job. I don't get paid until I get off."

"Nigga we ain't trying to pitch you no dope. We are trying to put some money into your pockets" Larry told him.

"Speak your mind then young blood."

"Can you turn a half a brick into twenty for us?"

"Can Michael Jackson moonwalk? Hell yeah, I can bring that back, that is nothing to ole Pete."

"Well when do you get off of work?"

"Shit let me do the math!" Pete started acting like he was figuring out a math problem in his head. "Forty grams that's damn near a month's pay at this raggedy ass spot, I'm off work right now!" He said as he dropped the soapy rag into the bucket and stepped out of the big jumpsuit.

"Let's go young ins."

They walked out of the carwash with the owner screaming after Pete, they all laughed as they walked up the hill.

They got back to the spot and pulled out the Pyrex, the soda, the mixer and the dope. They waited to see Pete perform his magic. Byron was smart, he took note of the whole process. He followed Pete from the table, to the sink, to the counter, the stove and back to the sink. After Pete cooled the Pyrex down he went back over to the counter, turned the bowl upside down and patted the bottom until a hard rock fell onto the counter.

Byron ran into the back bedroom and grabbed the scale. He sat the rock on it, and it weighed 630 grams. Byron and Larry gave each other dap. They paid Pete and told him that they would be back at him in about a week. Cook it up Pete left with a big smile on his face. He thought to his self, "Ole Pete is back!"

Byron and Larry set out to spread the word that they had that work. They walked through Morris Black selling anything from fifty dollar dubs and up. They walked up and down Woodland, then they went up to the Buckeye area promoting that they had weight. Once they got up they bought phones and passed their numbers out. Business picked up quickly. By the end of the week they were done. They counted out $22,000 dollars. They put eight grand up and took Rick his fourteen. Rick smiled when they came in.

"I knew that y'all could do it, I had faith in you boys. I am going to give y'all the other half and when y'all get through with that I am going to bless y'all with a whole one. Just don't get beside yourselves. I would hate to have to cut y'all down to size. Niggas that move too fast in the game, tend to get too big for their britches. Remember who is feeding you niggas and don't bite that hand. I will see you niggas next week."

They left and headed back to the spot.

"I can't wait to body that nigga!" said Larry.

"That nigga really thinks that he is dealing with some hoes."

"It's all good though, it's only a matter of time my nigga, only a matter of time" Larry said, then made a gun with his hand and pulled the trigger.

□

Rick was pulling out of his parking lot later that day. When he turned onto the street, he heard a police siren behind him. He looked into his review mirror and saw a gray Chrysler with a flashing light on its dashboard.

"Fuck do they want?" Rick thought to his self. He slid his gun into his stash box and pulled over.

Jenkins and Howard got out of their car and approached Rick's van. They split up, with Jenkins approaching on the driver's side and Howard coming up on the passenger's side. Rick rolled his window down as Jenkins approached. He immediately recognized him as the detective that had showed up in his hospital room last year.

"Mr. Spencer how are you?"

"I'm running late for a doctor's appointment, what's up?"

"Well we wanted to talk to you about what happened to you last year."

"Okay what's up?"

"Do you know a Marcus Mills, who is better known as Man?"

"No I do not know anybody by that name."

"That is odd because we have information that Marcus Mills, is Anthony Smith's cousin and was present the night that you and Anthony were shot."

"Look I don't know where you are getting your information from, but I do not know any Marcus Mills and I do not know anything more than what I told you last year except that I will be permanently confined to a wheelchair. Now if I am not under arrest for anything I need to be heading to my appointment."

"We wouldn't want to hold you up from your appointment now would we? You take care Mr. Spencer and make sure that you look both ways before crossing the street." Jenkins said then laughed.

Rick pulled off and Jenkins and Howard walked and got back into their car.

"If he wasn't confined to a wheelchair, I would of drug his ass out of that van and hauled him down to the station. He is lucky that I am close to retirement and do not need any blemishes in my file." Jenkins was saying it more to his self than anybody else.

Chapter 26

Spank was tired of feeling down and stressing. Tink was laid up in the hospital and Dame was in hiding fearing for his life. The crew was doing good and had things running smoothly. Spank decided that he was going to fly back to Miami and surprise Cherry. He intended to stay out there for a week or two, then come back and let his presence be felt, there would be no more hiding.

He met up with Kris and the rest of the crew at the stash house. He told them what his plans were. "Kris I want you to handle everything while I am gone. We are going to do it the same way. UPS the money and Hosea is going to have the shit delivered. Can y'all stay out of trouble while I am gone?"

"Me got you rude boy." Kris told him.

"Do any of y'all need me to bring y'all anything back?"

"Bring back some of that Miami weather back with you. It's too smoggy up here." said Rocky.

"I will bring some weather and some big booty gold teeth having strippers too!" Spank said and laughed.

"Speaking of big booty girls we are getting ready to go to a strip club, come with us Spank?"

"No, I got to get ready for my flight tomorrow."

"Rude boy, come now, go out with us and have some fun mon, we got you." Spank thought. "What the heck, it couldn't hurt to go out and have a few drinks."

"Alright I'm with y'all."

"Respect mon."

"Kris have you heard anything from Earn?"

"Him with the Rasta, him calls me every now and den. Me not know why he fall for dat girl. Maybe she put voodoo on him, him not same no more."

"It's all good, long as he is alright. Maybe one day he will come back to his senses. When I come back I am going to reach out to him. Real niggas do real things. We don't let no scandalous hoes come between us, let's roll to the club."

They all headed out to the cars and drove over to Monroe's. It was packed to be a Monday night. They paid the cover charge and went in. Instead of going to the bar they went and got two tables next to each other. They ordered drinks and exchanged knots of money for some ones.

Monroe's had a nice atmosphere. It was an upscale club with up-scale dancers. It did not have the bullet wounds and tattoo type of dancers. It had a mixed race of dancers. There were Black, White, Asian, and Mexican, you name it they had them.

The young thugs were not allowed in Monroe's. You had to be 25 and up to get in and no tennis shoes were allowed in the club. They had a live DJ playing the music. Girls in g-strings and garter belts moved throughout the club soliciting lap dances. Ten dollars got you a whole record.

For big spenders there was a VIP room, where all type of things took place. Spank and the crew were sipping their drinks when they announced the next dancer that was coming to the stage, her name was seduction. She came out onto the stage with the song *Shake it fast* by Mystical playing. Spank looked up at her on the stage and was memorized by her beauty. She stood about 5' 6"and had a Hershey chocolate complexion. Her eyes were slanted giving her a slight Asian ap-pearance.

Seduction moved her body in sync with the music. Her hips swayed back and forth. She seduced the audience. She made every individual in the audience feel like she was dancing specifically for them. To Spank it seemed like she was staring into his eyes as she danced. She had her back to the pole and did a full split facing the audience. Spank could not believe that he was getting rock hard inside of a strip club, while looking at a girl that was over twenty feet away from him.

Kris had to call his name three times, before he got Spank's attention, "Rude boy, she got you in a trance."

"Huh?"

"I called you like three times, the girl has your eyeballs." Spank tried to play it off.

"I had my mind somewhere else that's all."

"Whatever you say rude boy." Spank turned back to the stage, but to his disappointment the girl was no longer on stage. Nu-Nu and J-Bo were getting lap dances. A girl approached Spank and offered to give him a lap dance, and he refused. Spank looked at his watch and thought that he needed to be getting home. Just when he was about to tell the fellas that he was about to leave, the girl from the stage appeared right in front of him.

"You are not about to leave are you?" she asked him.

"Not now I'm not."

"Would you like a dance?"

"We can start there," she started dancing to Prince's song *Adore*. It was a slow song and she slowly and seductively danced for him. She straddled Spank facing him and grinded her pussy on his dick. Her lips softly brushed against his, as she put her arms around his neck. She locked eyes with Spank. To Spank it was like she was looking into his soul, it was as if she knew him.

"What is your name?" he asked her. She put her mouth to his ear and said, "Seduction!"

"No, your real name?"

"It is Nena."

"Nena what time do you get off?"

"What time do you want me to get off?"

"I'm ready to leave right now and trying to take you with me."

"First I would not just up and leave with you like that, that ain't me. Plus this is my job I could not just up and leave."

"Do you plan on working here forever?"

"Only until I can find something better."

"I'll tell you what, give me your number. I am about to head out of town tomorrow. When I come back we will discuss finding you a better job." Nena did not believe one word of what he was saying. Men sold her dreams every night trying to get some pussy. This guy did seem different to her though. It was something that made her give him her real number.

Ever since Sean had gotten killed. Nena had no one that she fucked around with steadily. She had tried to live a square life for a minute, after she had gotten shot. That life lasted about three months for her. She realized that the square life was not for her and decided to go back to doing what she did best, dancing.

This guy before her had something mystical about him.

"You're going to try to find me a better job and I don't even know your name."

"My name is Spank, I grew up down the way. Do a background check on me, and you will find out that I am trill. I got to get ready for this flight that I have to catch tomorrow. I will see you in a week or two." Spank told her as he stood up. He pulled a knot out of his pocket and peeled off a fifty dollar bill. He handed the money to her, told Kris and the rest of the crew that he was out, then headed to the door.

□

The next day Spank was on a plane headed to Miami. During the flight, Spank started to assess his life. He started thinking, "Yeah I got money, but what do I really have?" Spank knew that he had no stability in his life. He had no wife, no children. He had money, but did not own any businesses, nor did he have any investments. He felt that those may be the reasons why he didn't feel complete. He started drifting off, wondering what married life would be like. He thought to his self, "Could I really settle down? Maybe I should have a talk with Hosea, to see if he can give me some advice."

Spank's plane landed in Miami. He exited the plane, walked through the airport outside and hailed a taxi. He told the taxi driver to take him to the nearest jewelry store. He went into the store and bought a $10,000 engagement ring. Next, he had the cab driver take him to a flower shop. There he bought two dozen red roses. It was only 11AM in Miami. Spank thought that he would go and surprise Cherry. He was going to propose to her then take her out to brunch.

He had the cab driver take him out to his house in South Beach. Before he got out of the cab he paid the cab fare and tipped the driver fifty dollars, because he was in a good mood. He pulled out his house keys as he approached the house. He opened up the front door and stepped into the foyer. A delicious aroma filled his nostrils. The smell of fried bacon, eggs and pancakes hit him. He smiled at the thought of her making breakfast. He sat his things down, put the roses behind his back and headed into the kitchen.

When he got to the entrance, he saw Cherry at the stove cooking. She had on a red see through teddy. The teddy barely covered her naked ass cheeks. She took the pancakes out of the frying pan, and put them onto a plate. When she turned to sit the plate on the table, she saw Spank standing there. A look of horror appeared on her face, and she dropped the plate of hotcakes to the floor. Spank stood there confused by her actions. He wondered why did she look so terrified by is presence. All of a sudden Spank heard footsteps hurrying down the stairs, then a voice came, "Cherry are you alright?" The voice was coming towards the kitchen. Cherry was in a state of shock and could not respond. The man entered the kitchen wearing one of Spank's silk robes. He did not see Spank, as he rushed into the kitchen. As soon as the man went past, Spank reached out and. grabbed the back of the robe. He snatched the man up off of his feet, slammed him to the floor and started to pounce on him.

"No Spank! Stop it!" Cherry yelled at him. Spank was in a fit of rage. All of the stress that he had been experiencing lately, he took it all out on the man. Cherry being scared that Spank was going to kill the man rushed to the phone and called 911. She was talking to the dispatcher, when Spank snatched the phone out of the wall. He grabbed her by her throat, "Bitch! How could you do this to me huh? You got a nigga up in my house? I should kill you!" Cherry struggled for air and her eyes started bulging in their sockets. She desperately put her hands on top of his trying to pry his hands away from her neck. Spank released her neck and slapped her hard across her face knocking her to the floor.

"How could you Cherry? After all that I have done for you. How could you do this?" Cherry scooted back into the corner, trying to get as far away from him as possible. She looked over at Cody stretched out on the floor, and could not tell if he was dead or alive. Spank seen how she was looking at the man.

"What, you love that nigga?" Spank stormed over to the unconscious man and kicked him in the head repeatedly.

"Stop it Spank! You are going to kill him."

"I'm going to kill you too bitch, if you don't give me a good reason why you got this nigga up in my house?"

"It is over between us Spank. When I left Cleveland, I realized that we have no future together."

"Okay, fuck all of that, why are you here in my shit with this nigga?"
Cherry never got to answer that question, because of a loud banging
that was coming from the front door. Spank walked out of the kitchen,
and Cherry let out a sigh of relief. She had never seen Spank so angry
and did not know if she was going to live if no one interfered.

Spank walked to the door and opened it. Two police officers were at
his door.

"May I help you officers?"

"We got a call about a domestic dispute at this address."

"There has to be mistake officers. There has been no disturbance
here." Cherry appeared in the kitchen doorway.

"He is in here officers, I think he killed him." The officers quickly
drew their weapons on Spank. They put him up against the wall, patted
him down then cuffed him. They radioed for back up and paramedics to
be sent to the scene. After they had Spank secure one of the officers
rushed into the kitchen. He seen the man lying stretched out. He knelt
beside him and checked his pulse. The man had a steady pulse. The
officer figured that he may have just been knocked unconscious.

Back up arrived along with the paramedics. An officer took a statement from Cherry and the paramedics loaded the man onto the stretcher and carried him out to the ambulance. The police transported Spank
to jail.

Chapter 27

Fred was lying on his bunk at count time. As soon as count cleared the CO started doing mail call. Fred heard his name called. It surprised him because he usually only received mail around the holidays or his birthday. Usually it would be a card from his mother. He grabbed the letter from the CO and read the envelope. The letter was addressed from the Ohio Department of Corrections. Fred walked back to his bunk wondering what the letter could be about. He sat on his bunk opened the letter and read it. After he finished reading it, he had to reread it to make sure that he was reading it right. After reading it for a second time he decided to read it again for a third time. After that he knew that he was reading it correctly.

According to the Department of Corrections, due to overcrowding in the Ohio prison system, certain nonviolent inmates were being released from prison and placed in Community Correction Centers. The letter notified Fred that he had been one of the prisoners that were selected to serve the remainder of his time in a halfway house. He sat there not knowing exactly what that meant for him. Being in a halfway house was like still being in jail. They had strict rules that you had to follow. They gave you a certain amount of time to find a job, they took over half of your checks. Fred had planned on going unrestricted back to the streets and back into the game with the help of Keith.

He felt that he needed to talk to Keith as soon as possible. He wanted to make sure that there wasn't going to be any change of plans between them, now that he would be leaving earlier than they had expected.

Chow was called, and Fred headed towards the chow hall in search of Keith. He found Keith sitting in the chow hall, with a group of people surrounding him. It looked like they were celebrating something.

Keith looked up as he saw Fred approaching the table. "The game must need me Fred." Keith said when Fred got to the table. Fred thought that Keith was tripping. He thought that maybe he was just feeling his self.

"You sound like Jay-Z my nigga."

"By next week I'm going to be living like Jay-Z."

"Keith what the hell are you talking about?"

"By this time next week, I should be in the halfway house." Fred pulled his letter out of his pocket. "So you got one of these too?" Keith looked at the letter that Fred was holding.

"Damn nigga we are both about to be out of this bitch."

"Keith let me holla at you right quick, on some serious shit."

"Okay dawg, I will get up with y'all." Keith told everyone at the table. Him and Fred walked out to the yard and started circling the track.

"What's on your mind dawg?" Keith asked him.

"Do you really think being in a halfway house for seven months is a good look?"

"Fred, the halfway houses are overcrowded just like the prisons. They are pushing niggas out of there too. A week after we secure a job we will get pushed out of that bitch. I got my own businesses dawg, how hard can it be for us to get jobs?" Keith said to him with a smile on his face.

"I got you dawg, your boy Keith keeps his word. Within three months you are going to be riding through your hood in something with the roof missing." After hearing those words from Keith, Fred started to feel better. He started thinking that things wouldn't be so bad after all.

He went and called his mother to give her the good news and to tell her that he would be needing her to bring him some clothes down to the halfway house. After the call, he went and laid on his bunk. He fell asleep thinking about how he was about to get out and blow up.

Chapter 28

It had been over a week and nothing had developed for Dame. He could not find a way to get with Allen without there being any conflict. He still had not heard back from Spud concerning Spank's whereabouts. He was still held up in his house out in Mentor. Flip was being his eyes and ears in Cleveland.

Tink had put a dent in his pockets and he needed to get that money back. He went into his other stash and took out enough money to get some work. He thought to his self, "At a time like this I wish Disco was here." Disco had always been loyal to Dame. He trusted Disco with his life. He felt that everyone else that was surrounding him was doing it for the money. He felt that there was no true love around him, not even from Flip. One thing that he had learned since being in the game was that it loved no one. No matter how good you were to the game, it just would not give you any love back.

He called Spud and she answered, "Who is this?"

"This is Dame, I'm checking with you concerning what we talked about. You got something for me?"

"Spank seems to be missing in action. He ain't been around in about a week. I can give you the location of the stash house, but you might not want to go running up in there until spank is there. You could case it though. I'm sure that he is going to show up sooner or later."

"Yeah that will do, I will settle for whatever I can get right now."

"8436 E. 82nd St, it is the last house on a dead end street."

"And you are sure that this is Spank's spot?"

"I'm the one that rented it for him. Go over there you will see them gold front wearing niggas."

"Good looking Spud."

"Good looking don't pay the bills, I need ins!"

"Soon as I check out what you are telling me and confirm that the shit is real, I got you."

"Dame I will be waiting, serious business. Don't have me, get me." Spud told him then hung up.

☐

Allen and his crew had been trying to get a lead on Dame for almost two weeks. Allen and Pee Wee were riding around.

"I tried to tell Tink that he was making a mistake by letting that fat mother fucker live. Now he is lying up in the hospital fighting for his life!" Allen told Pee Wee.

"Yeah, I don't care how soft a nigga is, everybody has limits. If you push a nigga to the limit ain't no telling what he will do. You pin a seared man into a corner and he is going to fight his way out."

"I just hope that my nigga pulls through. He done been through a lot lately. His lady being raped, the loss of his seed and now he is laying up in the hospital in a coma, this shit is unreal."

"Now this sloppy fat mother fucker has gone into hiding. I say we go up to the Valley and start fucking up anybody that is associated with him. I'm talking about his friends, his workers even his fiends. Let's make it hard for that nigga to make any money."

Allen and Pee Wee got a couple of their other crew members together and started going up to the Valley terrorizing people. They would ride up on any group or single person that they see and jump out with pistols drawn and attack whoever it was that was in front of them.

Flip got word back to Dame about what was going on. Dame told Flip that it was time to resort to drastic measures. He instructed Flip to kidnap one of Allen's soldiers so that he could talk to him and send a message back to Allen. Flip was up for the challenge. He got two trigger happy niggas, that he knew took no shit and did anything for the right price.

Corey and Boom were referred to as the jump out boys. They were known to ride around in a van with a sliding side door. They would roll up on any block and jump out and snatch a person up off of their block in broad daylight.

Antonio was down with them. He was also their trusted driver. That day Flip was the tag along. He rode up in the front passenger's seat. He was to be the point out man. Telling Corey and Boom who to snatch. Antonio headed down to Longwood. Corey and Boom were in the back of the van clutching their weapons. They lived for the type of drama that they were about to experience. They got a high off of the things that they did. Yeah they put in work for the money, but they loved doing what they did for the thrill.

The van pulled into the Longwood Plaza and parked. The four of them sat in the van and watched the activity, and there was plenty of it

The Longwood plaza was a shopping center where the surrounding neighborhoods could shop for anything from clothes to food. It also had a Laundromat and a hair salon. The hair salon belonged to Coco. At one time the Nation of Islam had a hold on the Plaza. They used to patrol it making sure that no crime was committed. They often would clash with drug dealers that would try to set up shop inside of the plaza.

That had all changed a couple of years later. The Nation still had a restaurant in the plaza, but they no longer held any power over what went on inside of it. The plaza was full of drug dealers. The drug dealers were more into competition with each other than the actual stores were. When the police would storm through the plaza, the dealers would run up into the Muslim spot for shelter. Flip had one person in his sights, Ricardo. Ricardo stood outside of Coco's salon over seeing his workers.

"That's the nigga right there!" Flip told Corey and Boom as he pointed towards Ricardo through the front windshield.

"The nigga in the Polo Shirt?" asked Corey.

"Yeah that's him."

"You think them little niggas that he got with him got guns on them?" Boom asked.

"No, the guns are probably inside of the shop. The police ride through too much for a nigga to be stupid enough to have a gun on him."

"Okay, let's do this then." Corey said as he grabbed the door handle and opened the door. He opened the door but held it as if it was still shut. He held the door handle with his right hand and held his gun in his left hand. Boom was crouched down right beside him. Antonio pulled out of the parking space and circled the lot. When he felt that everything was a go he pulled the van to a stop right in front of Coco's shop. Corey quickly slid the van's door open and jumped out with his pistol raised, with Boom right at his side. Two youngsters that were with Ricardo seen the men and took off running without even informing Ricardo who had his back to the men talking on the phone. By the time that Ricardo felt a presence close up on him, he was being smacked in the same ear that he had the phone up to with a pistol.

The force from the blow caused a high pitch ringing noise in his ear. Corey grabbed Ricardo's upper body, while Boom grabbed his lower half. They carried him to the van and climbed inside with him. Flip reached back and slammed the side door shut. The people in the plaza looked on in amazement. Some wondered if that would be their last time seeing Ricardo.

Chapter 29

Byron and Larry were no longer walking. They went to a buy here pay here car lot and each bought a car. Byron had selected a 2008 STS Seville and Larry had gotten a 2007 Cadillac DTS. They road back to back up to the car wash on 93rd where cook it up Pete use to work. They had put Pete on a steady payroll, so he no longer had to wash cars.

They were each having their car detailed. They stood outside of the car wash enjoying the weather and plotting their next move.

"Nigga, we are doing the damn thing!" Byron said to Larry.

"Yeah, this is what's up, we got bitches all on our dicks. We ain't wanting for shit, yeah this the life."

"Wait until we pull up to the club in our shit, bitches is going to go crazy."

"Let's go to the rim shop next. I want to put some 24's on my shit!"

"That's a bet!" said Byron.

After getting their cars detailed, Byron and Larry drove down to 55th and Superior to Safeway rim and tire shop. They each had their car fitted with a set of 24" Lexani rims and tires. They then drove up to Morris Black to show their rides off to Rick. When they pulled into the parking lot, Rick was sitting in his wheelchair in front of his apartment.

When Byron and Larry hopped out of their cars, Rick had a look of pure hate plastered on his face. He started to feel that Byron and Larry were getting too big for their britches. Rick was more jealous than he was before he got paralyzed. He hated seeing two young niggas excel the way they were doing, even though he was the one who was actually putting them on. Instead of being proud of them he had started to despise them. To him, they were doing the things that he would be doing if he still had use of his legs. What really pissed him off was the fact that on several occasions he had caught Cynthia staring at Byron. She would have a look of admiration on her face.

Rick decided that it was time for him to start short stopping them. He was going to cut back the amount of dope that he was fronting them. He really wanted to keep them under his wing. He wanted to keep them as flunkies. They approached Rick and he put a fake smile on his face.

"I see you niggas shining. I have been thinking about me a Lac." Byron thought to his self "This nigga faking."

"Rick, we are ready for them two birds that you promised us!" Larry told him.

"My connect got me on hold, I ain't got nothing but a half for y'all."

"You got a half for both of us?" inquired Byron.

"No I got a half for y'all to split."

"Come on Rick, we will be done with that little shit in a couple of hours!"

"Fuck you want me to do? I ain't no damn magician. I been putting you niggas on. Damn! You niggas don't appreciate shit!"

"It ain't like that Rick, we are just trying to get this money while the getting is good. What if we find you another plug?" asked Byron.

"Fuck you mean find me another plug? Nigga I'm a G! I don't deal with just anybody. I am going to reach out to some other niggas that I know. If I come up, I'm going to get at y'all. If not then y'all are going to have to wait for my connect to get back right."

Rick's jealousy was making him think irrationally. He did not even take into consideration, that him short stopping Byron and Larry was also short stopping his self. They were actually putting more money in his pockets than they were making for themselves.

"Do you two want the half or what?"

"Yeah!" they both said in union. Rick spun his wheelchair around and headed into the house and they followed. They entered the house and Rick wheeled his self down the hall towards his bedroom. Cynthia was sitting on the couch, wearing a sheer night gown, watching television. She looked up and seen Byron standing there. She put a smile on her face and Byron winked at her. She positioned herself on the couch, so that Byron could see that she did not have any panties on. Byron's dick got hard from looking at her thick, black, hairy bush.

Rick came back rolling up the hallway and Cynthia quickly repositioned herself and went back to watching TV. Rick handed Byron the package.

"Take your time with it because I don't know when I will be on again."

"Yeah alright, let's go Larry." They walked out of the house.

"That nigga is trying to spoon feed us!" Byron told Larry.

"That nigga is jealous because we are coming up."

"It's about time we dead that fool. Soon as we get through with this shit, we are going to air his half a body ass out."

"We should put him in a wheelchair race."

"Fuck are you talking about Larry?"

"I say we take that nigga to the top of the hill on 116th, put his ass in the middle of the street, push him and let him race traffic down the hill, with two street lights to go through. I guess it would be like a game of chicken. Either he will survive or he won't." Larry said with a devilish grin on his face. Byron looked at him like he was crazy.

"Nigga I got to watch you, you are starting to think as sick as him."

"To be able to take a nigga's place you have to be able to think like them. Now come on and let's go and get this money!"

Chapter 30

Spank was in jail for three days before he decided to call Hosea. Hosea sent a bondsman to bail Spank out. He told the bondsman to wait for Spank to get released and to give him a ride home. Hosea stayed as far away from the police as possible.

When Spank was released and made it home. Hosea popped up on his doorstep. Spank had just finished showering and shaving when his doorbell rang. He slipped on a shirt and a pair of pants and headed down to answer the door. He approached the door, "Who is it?"

"It is me my friend, Hosea." Spank unlocked and opened the door. He stuck his hand out to shake Hosea's, "Thanks man, come on in." Spank said to him. Hosea entered the house and Spank led him into the living room. They both took a seat.

"So how are you my friend?"

"I'm good, I still can't believe that she had the audacity to bring another nigga into my home, that bitch has balls!"

"A woman is a very dynamic creature. She has many dimensions to her. They have good sides and they have bad sides. It all depends on how you treat them as to what side they choose to show you. Know this Spank, a scorned woman can be the most devious creature on the planet. They play the game better than any man ever could, because they use their minds instead of their emotions. Use this as a lesson, never take things for granted, and never think or assume that you know more about a person than you actually do know about that person."

"Hosea you are always talking in riddles. I'm from the hood, I don't be having time to try and decipher the shit that you be telling me."

"You have time Spank. You have plenty of time, you just get caught up racing against time. Slow down and take the time to think more. Start exploring all angles and not just one. Have you ever played chess?"

"No!"

"Well chess is a game of strategy. Two people are opponents, and they are trying to capture each other's king. To do that one has to out think the other. The one that studies the whole board and sees the outcome of his moves before he makes them usually wins. Why? Because they are not just taking in their next move they are also taking in what their opponent's next move will be. They are not trying to capitalize off of one move. They are taking their time to think two and three moves ahead of their opponent. You have good instincts Spank, but you need to start being a good strategist. Let me ask you this, what is your next move?"

"Shit, I don't know, what do you mean?"

"It is a simple question, I asked you what your next move is going to be. You were doing well here. Then you up and moved your whole crew to your hometown, and left your lady friend here like she would sit and wait forever for you, that did not materialize, so now what are you going to do next?"

"I am going back to Cleveland to finish up my business, and then I will figure out what I am going to do."

"Okay, but as I said while you are plotting one move, there is some-one out there that is two steps ahead of you so be careful my friend. I must leave now, I wish you well." Hosea left Spank's house.

Spank sat there trying to figure out exactly what Hosea was trying to get him to see. Spank had never been a thinker. He had always just trusted his instincts. He believed that all you needed to survive were good instincts. His instincts were telling him to get back to Cleveland to check on his money. He called the airport and booked a flight. He then went around the house making sure that everything was in order. Cherry had taken everything that he had bought her including all the jewelry and the car that he bought her. She had left his house keys on top of the kitchen counter. That was a chapter in his life that he knew was permanently closed.

☐

In Cleveland Coco and Silvia were sitting up in Tink's hospital room. Tink was still in a coma. The day before he was seen by a neurologist and was given a CAT scan. The scan indicated normal brain wave activity. The doctor informed Coco that when the body feels that it has healed itself enough, then maybe he would come out of the coma.

Coco started to wonder why they were having so much bad luck. She started to wonder if maybe it was karma. That old saying what goes around comes around. She knew that selling drugs was wrong and that it destroyed people's lives. First Linda, then her baby and now Tink.

Coco wished that she could trade it all back in, to have her friend, her baby and her man back. She sat by Tink's bedside and held his hand as he laid there unresponsive.

Silvia sat in a chair over in the corner. She felt bad for what her friend was going through. Allen appeared in the room.

"How are y'all holding up?" he asked them.

"We are okay." Coco replied.

"So what are the doctors saying?"

"They say that he has normal brain wave activity and that his body is still trying to heal itself. Have y'all found that nigga Dame yet?"

"No, that nigga must not be in Cleveland, but whenever he shows his face we are going to get his ass!"

"Have y'all seen Spank yet?" Silvia asked Allen.

"What do you mean have I seen Spank?"

"Shit, I thought that maybe you had run into him by now. I saw him at the Spy club a couple weeks ago."

"You mean to tell me that you saw Spank up here in Cleveland and you are just now saying something?"

"I been told Coco that I saw Spank. Matter of fact I told her the same day that Tink got shot."

"Shit! That could be the answer!" Allen was saying as he rushed out of the hospital room.

"You did try to tell me that you saw Spank. What if he is behind Tink getting shot? I could have prevented it!"

"Girl, don't go blaming yourself, you have already been through enough. You don't know that Spank was involved so don't go jumping to conclusions and end up stressing yourself out more than you already are."

"I guess you are right."

□

Flip, Corey and Boom had Ricardo tied up in the basement of a house. They were waiting for Dame and Spud to show up. They had called and let Dame know that they had Ricardo. Dame told him to take him to a house that he was getting remodeled down on Fleet Avenue. He told them that he was going to pick up Spud then shoot down there.

Dame stopped and picked Spud up. He told her that he had one of Allen boys and he wanted her to tell him what was up, so that he could relay it to Allen. The first thing that Spud asked about, when Dame told her of his plans was for some money. Dame knew that she was thirsty. He had brought ten stacks with him. He tossed it to her and told her that he would give her another ten stacks when everything was settled.

They arrived at the house and went down into the basement. The last time that Ricardo had seen Dame he was standing inside if his living room holding his family at gun point. Ricardo just knew that Dame had him kidnapped to get revenge for what he had done. Ricardo was hoping that he just made it out alive, being as they did not harm Dame or his family.

Dame stood in front and spoke, "I know that you think that I had them bring you here to do you harm, but that is not the case. I had them bring you here, so that you can go back and tell Allen what the hell is really going on. We have been getting hit on both sides, and we have been pointing the finger at each other. I have found out that someone has been doing shit in a manipulative way, so that we would think that each other were behind the shit. That person is Spank."

"Ain't nobody going to believe that shit!" Ricardo told him.

"That's why I brought her. This is Spud and Allen is familiar with her. I am going to let her tell you the story that she told me." Dame turned to Spud, "The floor is yours."

"Spank was in Miami for a year plotting get back. He came back about two months ago with a crew of niggas from down there. Two of them were Jamaicans. Spank wanted to get back at Tink for taking his spot, and he wanted Dame for siding with Tink. He wanted to do things in a manipulative way so that Dame and Tink would point the finger at each other, obviously it worked."

"So where is the nigga Spank at now?" asked Ricardo.

"Like I told Dame, he has been missing for about a week now, but also as I told Dame, I know where the stash house is. His crew is staying there. Whenever Spank pops back up that is where he will be."

"Okay Dame, you done had her tell me all of that, what happens now?"

"You are free to go, I just want you to tell Allen what you have found out. Give him this number to contact me, so we can get together and figure out how to handle the situation."

"Flip you can cut him loose and take him back to where you got him from."

Flip untied Ricardo and Dame handed him a paper with a number on it. They took Ricardo back out to the van. This time they allowed him to ride in the front passenger's seat. They took him back down to the plaza and dropped him off back in front of Spud's shop. The same people that watched in amazement when he got snatched off of the block looked on in amazement again, as Ricardo freely jumped out the front seat of the van and walked into Coco's shop.

Ricardo entered the shop and went straight to the back office. He picked up the phone and called Allen. He told Allen how he had been kidnapped and that he needed to see him to tell him what he had found out. Allen told him to sit tight, that he was on his way.

Chapter 31

Spank caught a plane back to Cleveland. When he touched down he had a new motto, if you wasn't down with his click, fuck you. The hiding was over. He was about to make his presence be felt in the city. After Spud, Earn and Cherry he felt that it was time to go back to the old Spank. He decided that they were going to the club that night.

Kris was at the airport to pick him up. Spank got into the car and let his seat back.

"How was your trip back rude boy? You and your lady friend have fun?"

"Fuck no! That bitch had another nigga up in my house. He was wearing my robe. I kicked both of their asses and ended up being locked up for three days."

"Girls don't play games like that mon!"

"Somebody should have told her that."

"That is why me no trust woman, me fuck dem and dat it, me don't love dem."

"I guess some of us have to learn the hard way."

"Where we go now?"

"Let's go and get everybody and go back to that bar that we went to the night before I left. I got someone that I want to see up there."

"Girl that had your eyeballs, be careful dis time."

"No doubt." They went and picked up the rest of the crew and headed over to Monroe's. They got there, went inside and copped two tables that were up front by the stage. That night was less crowded than the time they were before. Spank did not care he was really there for one reason. He wanted to see Nena again. He did not know why it seemed that he was always attracted to strippers. Nevertheless, he could not figure out why he thought that he could treat them any differently from what they really were.

Spank thought he had power over people. He thought that his mystical powers could change anyone, even a hoe into a housewife.

They were in the club an hour before Nena appeared. As soon as she took the stage, she locked eyes with Spank. While she did her whole routine, she never took her eyes off of him.

Spank stared back at her, knowing that he would be fucking her that night. After she finished her dance she collected her money, left the stage and headed straight towards Spank. She stopped in front of him.

"I heard some good things about you and I heard some bad things about you. I even heard some things that were hard to believe."

"So, you did do a check up on me huh?"

"Yeah I did, it is something about you that made me know that I would be seeing you again. I wanted to find out who it is that I was going to be dealing with."

"Okay, tell me one of the good things that you heard about me?"

"I heard that you are about your business."

"Give me one of the bad things."

"That you are very violent and have a quick temper."

"And the unbelievable things that you heard?"

"That you got chased out of your hood and out of town."

"And do you believe that?"

"If it is true, they couldn't have chased you too far, this is my second time seeing you. Plus you seem like the type that won't run from anything."

"With all that being said, you are leaving with me tonight right?"

"I guess I am but, I got one more set to perform then I can leave."

"I will be right here." Nena walked off. Spank felt heat on the back of his neck like someone was trying to burn a hole through him with their eyes. He turned around and seen Earn and Jamaican Mark sitting at the bar staring at him. Spank had heard all of the rumors about the reputation that they had earned. They were being referred to as the notorious duo. The word was that they were fronting young boys dope and if they came up even a dollar short that they would make examples out of them. They would either beat their hands with a hammer or burn them with a hanger. The rumors also said that they were bullying people up off of their own blocks. They would give them two options, work for them or get off the block. They were forcing people that actually hustled and lived on the blocks for years, to get down or be put down.

Spank wondered what they were up to. Earn sat there staring at Spank for no apparent reason. He had started to despise Spank. He thought that Spank wasn't worthy of the position that he had. He did not think Spank was a real killer.

Mark was all in his ear. "American got no heart. Him still scared of the white man. Him act tough standing behind him crew. We take dem down." His words gassed Earn up. He really only had love for one person that was in Spank's click. That was Kris and that was only because he was half Jamaican.

Earn had been drinking and smoking and he was feeling himself.

"Me show Spank who real don dodda is, him pussy crying over bleeding cunt." Earn pushed his self up off of his stool and headed over to spank's table. Mark was right on his heels. Mark loved trouble and would instigate it at any chance he got. Spank saw them approaching. He already had his mind made up, that if Earn tried to flex in any type of way, that he was going to smash him.

Spank nudged Kris to get his attention. He pointed at Earn and Mark headed their way. Kris looked and saw Earn. He only seen Earn once since he had defected their camp. To him they had no beef. He did not know exactly what had gone down between Earn and Spank, but he knew that it involved that bitch Spud.

To Kris the two biggest things that niggas kill each other over were money and bitches. Sometimes bitches cause more deaths than money. Earn reached their table and tried to stare Spank down. Spank stayed seated, he looked up into Earn's face.

"What's up screw face?"

"You try to disrespect me botty boy. You no killa, me killa." Kris stood up.

"Earn come on mon, we no disrespect you. We enjoy music and girls."

"Spank your leader, him pussy. Ya whole crew is pussy, you only half Jamaican me 100% real Jamaican don dodda. You side with American pussy."

"Earn respect mon."

"No, fuck respect!" Spank said as he stood up.

"Earn I been letting the little shit that you and Rupaul over there have been doing slide, fucking with my money and shit. You done let that shit go to your head. You disrespect me again, and I'm going to cut your dick off and stick it in your mouth."

"Who you call Rupaul?" Mark asked stepping forward. The rest of Spank's crew stood to their feet.

"I'm talking to you bitch!" Spank said. Since Earn was the closes to him, he took off on him. He caught him flush on the chin, sending him crashing straight to the floor. Spank still had a lot of pent up frustration inside of him and he started releasing it on Earn. He started stomping him to the head. Jamaican Mark tried to step forward with a knife in his hand, but fell to the floor next to Earn after Nu-Nu hit him on top of the head with a Corona bottle. He too got stomped out before the bouncers could get Spank and his crew out of the club.

Spank and his crew left out of the club, but they did not leave. They walked across the street to their cars. Spank just leaned up against his. About five minutes later Nena exited the club. She saw Spank leaning on his car and headed across the street towards him. She told him, "I think you should get out of here, those guys are hurt pretty bad, the owner called the paramedics and the police."

"Are you going with me?"

"I'm right here ain't I?"

"You got a little sass in you huh? I like that. Nu-Nu and Rocky got into the car with Kris and J-Bo. Nena got into the car with Spank. He did not know her well enough to take her to his house or the stash spot, so he headed to a hotel.

He took her to the Hyatt Regency in downtown Cleveland. He reflected on his new motto, "Fuck them and play them for what they are worth. No more trying to wife a bitch, at least not a hoe that I met in a strip club."

Chapter 32

Earlier Allen had picked Ricardo up from Coco's shop, Ricardo had hopped into the car.

"Do you remember, Close Encounters of the Third Kind?" Ricardo asked Allen.

"Rick, what the fuck are you talking about?"

"This movie where some aliens came to earth and kidnapped some people."

"Nigga have you been smoking water or something?"

"No nigga, I'm just trying to make a comparison. Some niggas came down to the plaza and kidnapped me. They took me to some basement, where the nigga Dame popped up with this chick name Spud. Dame had her tell me this story about Spank and some niggas from Miami being behind all that has been going on. Then they brought me back down here and drop me back off so that I could tell you what they told me. Now if that ain't no alien type of shit, I don't know what is!"

"So it's true then?" Allen said to his self.

"Fuck you, talking about it's true then? Nigga you been smoking water?"

"The bitch Silvia said that she seen Spank in the club, the same night that Tink got shot!"

"I guess they ain't lying then. The hoe Spud say she know where their stash house is at. Dame gave me a number and told me to tell you to call him. He says he wants y'all to join forces so that y'all can go after the real enemy."

"I should have known that Dame's bitch ass was too soft to be behind all of this shit. He wants us to join forces with him, this ain't no fucking military. We don't need to join up with them fucking niggas to see nobody."

"So you ain't fucking with him?"

"Give me that nigga's number, I'm going to holla at him." Ricardo handed Allen the paper with the number on it.

Allen called Dame and he answered, "Who dis?"

"It's Allen nigga!"

"Oh, what's up Al Man, I hope that you are ready to dead all of this bullshit. I told y'all that I didn't have anything to do with any of that shit. That nigga Spank's punk ass is behind everything. I say we get together and get at that nigga."

"Dame ain't nobody fucking with your soft ass or them niggas that you run with. We been terrorizing them hoe ass Valley niggas. Nigga you do what you got to do and we are going to handle our own. Who-ever get him, get him. Have that bitch Spud holla at me though. Tell that bitch I said to get with me ASAP. Tell her I said get at me before I have to get at her and if I have to do that it ain't going to be nothing nice!"

"I will deliver the message to her."

"Yeah you do that!"

"So, Al is everything good between us?"

"Go ahead and breathe for now nigga. If this shit doesn't pan out though, you are only going to have a few breaths left." Allen hung up the phone on Dame. Ricardo looked over at him.

"You're a cold nigga Al."

"It's a cold world nigga, but believe shit is about to heat up. So don't let your ass get kidnapped again. Stay strapped you feel me?"

"Yeah I feel you!"

"I hope that you got some change on you."

"Why is that?"

"Because I'm about to drop you off at the bus stop, I got to make a move" Allen told him as he pulled over to the curb. Ricardo just shook his head and then got out of the car.

Allen pulled off, and dialed a number on his phone. A female answered, and he told her, "I'm on my way, meet me in the front lot."

"Okay, I'm about to leave out right now." The female hung up the phone, grabbed her purse and walked to the front of the house.

"Rick, me and Tiny are about to go to the Club Center. I'm about to walk down to her house."

"Don't have your ass out all night, and you bet not come back in here with no dick on your breath!"

"Boy, you are always tripping." Cynthia told him as she headed out the door. She walked up to the front parking lot and waited on Allen. Fifteen minutes later he pulled into the lot. Cynthia got into the car with him and he pulled off.

"When are you going to get it over with? I'm tired of that mother fucker, he makes me sick?"

"What is he working with?"

"I think that nigga just copped three bricks. He is fronting these two young niggas, but since they been coming up he been short stopping them. So we best get what he got now, so I can get away from his cripple stanking ass!"

"Don't worry I will get it taken care of, in the next day or two, right now I'm trying to get up in that pussy!" Allen told her as he headed to the motel.

□

Byron and Larry were getting ready to go and take care of some business.

"You got the money?" Byron asked Larry.

"Yeah I got it."

"Did you talk to Cynthia?"

"Yeah, I acted like I was trying to creep with her, but she told me that she was about to go to a club with her girl."

"She better not be there, I would hate to have to dead something as beautiful as she is."

"Don't worry, she ain't going to be there, you got your strap?"

"I got my strap and this baby Louisville slugger."

"What the fuck do you got a bat for?"

"I want to see if he really don't have no feelings in his legs, plus he don't deserve no quick death. All the shit he has done and how he done played people, he is going to pay!" Larry told Byron.

"Make sure that you got your gloves on, we can't leave any prints."

"I got you!" They left out of the house and walked through the Black. They did not need to drive a car, because they were only going a couple of yards over. They each had on black Dickie outfits. They went up to Rick's door and rang the doorbell. He did not answer after three rings, Byron started banging on his door. All of a sudden they heard noises that sounded like something was bouncing off of the walls.

"Hold the fuck up I'm coining!" Rick said as he bumped into the walls and the furniture. Being in a rush to see who the fuck it was banging at his door, he did not turn any of the lights on. He bumped into everything that was in his way as he headed to open the door.

"Who the fuck is it?"

"It's Byron,"

"Is you niggas crazy? Somebody better be dying the way you niggas banging on my damn door this time of night." Byron laughed and said to his self, "If you only knew." Referring to the comment that Rick had just made about somebody better be dying. Rick unlocked the door and opened it, with a pistol lying in his lap.

"Fuck you niggas want?"

"We come to bring you your cash."

"You mother fuckers couldn't wait until the morning, to bring my shit?" They stepped inside and closed the door. Larry pulled out the money.

"We are out we need some more work."

"I told y'all that my connect got me on hold, you niggas don't listen."

"Come on Rick, I know you got something!" Byron said.

"You little niggas are greedy, y'all are too ambitious. Y'all want to be me, y'all can never be me. Without my legs I'm still better than both of you niggas put together!"

Larry stepped forward and threw the money into Rick's lap. He quickly pulled out the bat and hit Rick on the side of his head. Rick hands instantly went to his face. Larry pulled him out of the wheelchair, picking up Rick's gun as it fell to the floor.

"Yeah nigga, you ain't got no feelings in your legs, but that dome shot fucked you up didn't it?" Larry said then laughed.

"Gone to the back and get that shit my nigga, I got this." Byron headed down the hall to Rick's bedroom saying to his self, "That nigga Rick created a monster, I feel sorry for him!"

Larry asked Rick, "Is you ready to suffer my nigga?" Larry took the bat and started beating Rick from the knees down. He busted Rick's knee caps and broke his legs in many places. Rick did not feel the pain, but he did feel the pressure.

"I put you niggas on, why are y'all taking advantage of a handicap nigga?"

"When you was busting your gun you wasn't handicap, you wasn't handicap when you was treating us like lames, you wasn't handicap when you killed my nigga Mookie. Take this shit like a man nigga!" Larry started beating Rick in his rib cage and his chest area. He broke his rib cage in several places, he cracked his chest plate and broke his collar bone.

Rick was slipping in and out of consciousness, "Come on Rick don't die on me this fast, stay alive nigga, you ain't no fun!"

Byron came back up the hall carrying two bags. One was small and the other one was large.

"Jackpot my nigga, this nigga was holding. We are on dawg, let's go."

"I got to finish what I started, take a seat and enjoy the show." Larry said with a deranged look on his face.

"Larry, just give that nigga one to the dome and let's get out of here."

"Just let me break his face right quick." Larry started hitting Rick in the face and head with the bat.

"This is for Mookie nigga!" Blood spatter was going everywhere as he broke Rick's jaws and nose. He also knocked out all of his front teeth and bashed his head in. Rick was not breathing anymore. Byron had seen enough. He stepped forward and grabbed Larry.

"That's enough dawg." He had to snap Larry out of his zone. Byron shot Rick twice in the head for safe measures, then they left Rick's house. They headed back the way from which they had come. They got back to the house. Byron went into the kitchen and dumped the bags out on the table. The large bag was filled with loose money. It was so much money that some of it fell over onto the floor. Out of the smaller bag fell three wrapped bricks of cocaine.

"I knew that bitch ass nigga was holding out on us. Talking about his connect. This nigga had enough dope to be a connect his self." Byron said.

"We know what we are working with on the dope side, so let's count this money up." Larry said. They pulled out two kitchen chairs, sat down and began counting the money.

☐

Cynthia got in about 2:30 in the morning. She put her key in the door and was surprised to find that the door was already unlocked. She found that strange, because of how paranoid Rick was. She stepped inside of the house and flicked on the light. She almost fainted when she saw the gruesome sight. Rick was lying dead on the floor. She could tell that he was dead from the way that his body was twisted up. Plus he looked like he had every bone in his body broken.

Cynthia tiptoed down the hall to the bedroom. She looked into the room and saw that it had been ransacked. She entered the room and went to Rick's stash spots. They both were empty, his stash had been taken. She figured that she and Allen had waited to late or that he had double crossed her.

Cynthia did not love Rick nor respect his gangster, as he thought. She was with him to get his money and split it with her real man, Allen. She had been fucking with Rick for six months at Allen's urging. They were waiting for the right time to get him. Allen was at Rick ever since Sean had gotten killed. He felt that the reason Sean was killed originated back to the shit that Rick had tried to pull.

Cynthia started to wonder if Allen had double crossed her. Did he trick her out of the house, so that he could have somebody run up in there? She thought to herself, "Would he actually play me like that?" She stepped outside and pulled the door shut. She called Allen's phone. He answered, "You miss me already?"

"What type of shit are you on Al?"

"Whoa, whoa little momma, talk to me, I'll talk back."

"You had somebody run up in here, without telling me?"

"Cynt, I don't know what you are talking about, I swear I don't!"

"Well you can cancel that shit that you had planned, I just found Rick in here beaten to death and all the money and the dope is gone."

"So, where are you at now?"

"I'm sitting out on the porch."

"Look you got to play it all the way out now. Everybody knows that you were fucking with the nigga, so you can't just up and bounce. Call 911 and report that shit, when the police get there put your best game face on!"

"I been fucking this crippled, stanking mother fucker for six months for nothing. Now I'm about to have to put up with all these questions and shit."

"Don't worry Cynt, I got you. I ain't going to ever let you be fucked up."

"You better not, let me go so I can call the damn police!"

"Alright, call me when everything is done."

"Yeah, alright!" Cynthia hung up from Allen, then called 911. She did her best acting, crying hysterically telling the dispatcher that she had just come home and found her boyfriend beaten to death.

Within twenty minutes, the front of Rick's apartment was flooded with police cars. There were uniform police and there were plain clothes police. They had the coroner and the crime scene investigation unit. People had started to file out of their apartments to see what was going on. They watched as Rick's body was brought out covered in a white sheet and put into the back of the coroner's car.

Jenkins and Howard were inside of the house questioning Cynthia. She could not provide them with much information concerning the murder. They asked her had anything been taking from the house. She told them that the bedroom had been ransacked.

They proceeded back to the bedroom. They searched it and found guns all over it. In the closet they found a pump shot gun. In the dresser drawer they found a .357 magnum, and under the mattress they found a Tech 22.

"Look what I found!" Howard called out to Jenkins. Jenkins walked over and looked at the weapon.

"You think this could be it?"

"That is my guess."

"If this is the weapon, for a man that was paralyzed, Mr. Spencer was a very active man."

"Did you see the way his body was broken up?" asked Jenkins.

"Whoever killed him did it in a fit of rage. If he is tied to all of those killings, ain't no telling who could have done this to him."

"The last time that we saw him, he was on his way to a doctor's appointment. I wonder if the doctor advised him that he had less than a week to live." Jenkins said.

After they wrapped the crime scene up, they headed downtown. They wanted to personally deliver the Tech 22 to the crime lab for testing.

Chapter 33

Spank and Nena left the hotel that morning and Spank took her to breakfast. They went to the Best Steak House and had steak, eggs and hash browns. They sat and talked as they ate.

"So Spank you are from down the way. I had a close male friend that was from down the way."

"You said he was from down the way, what happened to him?"

"He got killed."

"Oh yeah, what was his name?"

"Sean."

"Sean who?"

"Sean Oliver."

"Get the fuck out of here! Sean was my nigga, he was part of my click."

"I was with him when they tried to rob him up in Morris Black?"

"You the one that got shot and was up in the hospital?"

"Yeah that was me."

"That's crazy, it's a small world. Sean was my right hand man, I miss my nigga."

"I miss him too, he was a real nigga. Now that I think about it, he did use to mention the name Spank a lot."

"You are like family now, you stood up for my nigga on some real shit. May my nigga rest in peace, at least he knows that you are in good hands. Come on I got to take you home. I got to get out in these streets and make moves."

Spank dropped Nena off and headed to the stash house. Earn and Mark had to call and have someone pick them up from the hospital.

Earn had to get his jaw wired shut. Spank's blow to his chin had fractured his jaw in three places. His jaw was going to be wired for six to eight weeks. Mark had to get twelve stitches in his head, the blow from the Corona bottle split his scalp to the white meat and his eye socket was fractured too.

Mark's cousin Isaiah picked them up from the hospital and took them back over to Monroe's to get their cars. When they got up to Dailey's, Mark told two of his cousins to get strapped because they were going to settle up with the guys that had jumped them. Mark and Earn got strapped, and along with Mark's two cousins they hopped into a Nissan Maxima. Earn directed them down to the stash house. Nu-Nu, J-Bo and Rocky were all sitting on the front porch smoking a blunt. Kris was inside of the house cooking dope.

J-Bo looked up and saw an all-black Maxima with tinted windows driving slowly down the street towards them.

"Look at that car creeping down the street." Rocky and Nu-Nu looked at the car slowly coming down the street.

"Don't trip act normal." J-Bo said as he nonchalantly got up and went into the house, he went into the kitchen and told Kris, "There is a car creeping down the street. They could be trying to rob us."

"Okay, me get big gun!" Kris said and headed into the bedroom. J-Bo went into the living room and grabbed three guns from under the seat cushion. He went back outside and sat back down in the chair. He tossed a gun to Nu-Nu and one to Rocky. The Maxima rode past the house and was now at the end of the street turning around, because it was a dead end street. All three of them stood up and walked off of the porch in different directions. Kris came out of the side door and was standing in the driveway. The car started back towards them. The windows of the car were down. All of a sudden the car sped up heading for the house, with guns sticking out of the windows. Before the car could get up on them they all started firing at the car. Automatic fire came from the back window of the car. J-Bo, Nu-Nu and Rocky all took cover. Kris ran out of the driveway when the car was almost in front of the house.

"Bombo blood clot he yelled!" as he opened fire with the Ak47. Bullets from the Ak47 hit the driver and the person that was shooting out of the back window. The driver had slumped over the wheel, but the car was still moving. All four of them converged on the car raining bullets on it from every angle. The dead weight of the driver's foot had the car moving at high speed.

Spank turned onto the street and heard rapid gun fire. Before he had a chance to figure out what was going on there was a car coming directly at him at a fast rate. He quickly swerved to get out of the car's way. When he straightened his car out he saw Kris running behind the car shooting an AK47. He saw his other three crew members running back towards the house. He heard a loud crash and looked into his mirror and saw that the Maxima had run up on the sidewalk and crashed into a light pole.

Kris ran up on the car and continued to shoot inside. Spank yelled out of his window for Kris to come on. Kris took off running towards Spank's car. He got in and Spank sped towards the house. When Spank got to the house, he jumped out of his car and ran into the house. The other crew members were already running around grabbing things that they needed. Spank said, "Get the dope and the money, and fuck everything else. Hurry up we got to get out of here before the police come!"

They grabbed the dope, the money and anything else that they could easily snatch up on their way out of the door. They all jumped into their cars. Spank was the lead car. He looked over at Kris who was still sitting there clutching the Ak47.

"Kris put that shit down, lay it on the floor!" Spank told him. Spank jumped on the freeway, since him and Spud had fell out he had no choice but to take them out to his house in Euclid.

Chapter 34

Fred and Keith were sent to the halfway house down on 18th and Euclid. It housed men and women. Fred was assigned to the third floor, while Keith was assigned to the fourth.

The next day after they got there, Fred was called in to see his counselor. The counselor explained to him all of the rules. He told him that he would have to be there for 48 hours before he was given an 8 hour pass to go look for a job. He advised him that he had a curfew that he was not allowed to possess a cell phone or own a car while he was in the halfway house. He told Fred that he only had one shot. He told him that the first time that he messed up that he was sending him back.

Later that day Fred was sitting in the cafeteria with Keith.

"Man my counselor is a bitch. He threatened to send me back the first time I make a mistake." Fred told Keith.

"Fuck that counselor, be easy we will be out of here in two weeks. I already got shit lined up. The first time that we get our passes we are going up to my shop, I got us trust me."

Two days later Fred and Keith got 8 hour passes to go and look for a job. They left out of the halfway house at eight in the morning. They walked around the block and stood on the corner for about five minutes before a silver GS Lexus pulled to a stop in front of them. "Come on!" Keith told Fred as he hopped into the front seat. Fred climbed into the back seat and was surprised to see that it was a girl driving the car. He could only see a side view of her, but he could tell that she was bad. He looked at her hands gripping the steering wheel and saw big ass diamonds on her fingers.

"Go to the house first, I got to get me some of that pussy and call one of your girls to come over and hook my nigga up!" Keith told the girl.

The girl pulled out a phone and dialed a number, and then she started talking into the phone, "A Sabrina they just gave Keith and one of his boys eight hour passes from the halfway house. Keith wants you to come over and hook his boy up, Okay hold on." The girl turned around and looked at Fred then turned back and started talking into the phone again, "Yeah he alright, Okay meet me at my house?" The girl ended the call.

"Fred this my girl Ramona, she is my down chick. Her girl Sabrina is down too. She is a bad bitch, so don't get shy when you see her." Fred sat back cheesing. He thought to his self, "This nigga really got the juice, he had one bad bitch pick us up and another one that is about to meet up with us to give me a shot of ass, with no questions asked, that's what's up!"

Ramona drove out to her house in Cleveland Heights. She pulled into a single family brick house. A Dodge Charger pulled in right behind her. They got out of the car and Ramona went to go unlock the door. Sabrina stepped out of her car with a large coach bag on her shoulder. Fred looked at her and felt star struck. Sabrina was a complete replica of Halle Berry. She fit the description all the way down to her build. She walked up and gave Keith a hug.

"Hey Keith?"

"What's up Brina, this my nigga Fred. He's fresh out and he gets money, do him right!" Sabrina looked Fred up and down.

"Shit! He better do me right!" They headed into the house.

"Y'all can use the other room." Keith said as he trotted up the stairs.

Sabrina turned to Fred, "You got any protection?"

"Nope, this my first time being free in eighteen months." Sabrina went into her purse and pulled out a box of rubbers, she sat her purse back down on the couch and said, "Come on!" as she led the way upstairs. They walked past the first bedroom, the door to the room was opened, and Fred looked in. He was surprised to see that Ramona was ass naked giving Keith head, while he was on the bed reclined back on his elbows. Keith winked at Fred when he saw him looking.

"I guess you want some of that?"

"Huh?" Fred responded.

"Head nigga, you want your dick sucked don't you?" Fred did not know what to say as they continued on to the next bedroom. Once inside of the room Sabrina started stripping out of her clothes. She did not even bother with shutting the door.

"Nigga what are you waiting on, come up out of that shit! I hope you ain't scared." Fred thought to his self, "This chick is wild." He had never met a girl as pretty as she was and was so outgoing. He wasn't going to let her punk him. He took his clothes off, he took off everything, including his socks. Sabrina stood there watching him strip with her hands on her hips. When Fred was completely naked she said, "Damn nigga! I should be the one scared of you, holding dick like that. I hope it ain't no waste. Most of you fully equipped niggas don't know how to use your shit."

Sabrina sat on the bed, "Come over here, and let me taste it." Fred walked over and stood in front of her. She reached out with her hand and grabbed his dick. Using her hand she pulled his dick up to her mouth. She engulfed him as she used her fingers to play with his balls. Fred had to reach out with both of his hands and put them on Sabrina's shoulders so that he could keep his balance.

The head that she was giving him was making him lightheaded. Sabrina stopped giving him head and said, "Since you're just getting out, I'm going to let it be about you, but next time you are going to have to return the favor and suck this pussy." She tore open one of the packs of rubbers. She took the rubber out of the pack and put it into her mouth. She used her mouth to put the rubber on Fred's dick.

She scooted back on the bed, laid down, grabbed her knees and bent them back to her chest. She had them spread wide and used her hands to hold them in place. Fred climbed on top of her. He lined his dick up with her pussy and pushed it in. Fred hadn't had pussy in so long that he just wanted to savor it. He sunk all the way in and just laid in her pussy for about three minutes. He enjoyed the feeling of his dick being in her pussy.

Fred started fucking Sabrina. He could tell that she was enjoying the feeling from the way that her eyes were rolling into the back of her head.

Fred wasn't trying to make love he was trying to fuck. He started pounding Sabrina. She kept holding her knees back to her chest. She started to egg Fred on.

"Come on nigga beat this pussy up, work that back. Shit yeah nigga, that's it!" Fred went into a frenzy. His whole body was wet and he was breathing like he had just finished running ten laps around a track.

Sabrina grunted like an animal. She let her legs go and pulled Fred into her as far as he could go. She started cumming and her orgasm triggered Fred's.

After Fred was finished he got up out of Sabrina. He knew that he and Keith needed to get going. Sabrina got up, went to him and pulled the rubber off of his dick.

"Let me go flush these babies down the toilet!" she said as she walked out of the bedroom naked headed to the bathroom. Fred started getting dressed. Sabrina walked back into the room and started getting dressed also. She looked at Fred and said, "Nigga if you are about your business in the streets the way that you are in the bed, I can fuck with you. I'm going to give you my number."

After they both got finished getting dressed they headed downstairs. Keith was sitting on the couch with Ramona smoking a blunt. Keith watched them come down the stairs. He exhaled some smoke and said, "Brina did you take care of my dawg?"

"Ask him."

"She look out for you dawg?"

"Yeah, she looked out, but what is you doing smoking. You know that they are probably going to piss test us when we get back."

"I got that covered, it ain't nothing that a little gold seal can't handle. All I got to do is stop at a GNC store, you want a hit?"

"No I'm good!"

"Okay let's roll we only got a couple hours left." They all left the house. Sabrina gave Fred her number, before she took off. Ramona drove them up to Keith's auto repair shop. They got there and Keith took Fred in. They entered the shop and Keith headed to the back office. Keith opened the door to the office and Jim looked up from the desk. A smile appeared on Jim's face as he stood up from the desk. Him and Keith approached each other and gave each other a hug.

"I'm glad you're home."

"I'm glad to be home!" Keith said.

Jim was Keith's partner. They were partners in legal and illegal businesses. Jim was to Keith what Slim was to Baby of Cash Money. While Keith was flashy, Jim played the background. There was nothing flashy about him.

"So how has business been doing?" Keith asked him. Jim did not respond he just looked at Fred. Keith picked up the hint.

"Oh! He cool, this my nigga Fred, he's off of Buckeye. He is going to be our man up there." Jim proceeded to talk, "We have been doing well, and we just got another shipment last week."

"What about the car?"

"It is out in the shop, come on I will show you." They all headed out into the shop. Over in the corner was a car that was covered up. When they reached the car Jim pulled the cover off. Underneath it was a 500SL convertible Mercedes.

"The keys are in it." Jim told Keith. Keith got into the car and started it up and let the top down. He told Fred to get in.

"Ain't no plates on it."

"That's okay open the garage door." Jim opened the door and Keith pulled out of the shop. He pulled up next to Ramona, "Follow me so the police can't get behind me." he told her as he sped out of the lot. Unbeknownst to them the feds were taking pictures of them as they pulled out in the Benz. Jim may not have been flashy, but he had popped up on the feds radar after an informant had turned over his name to them.

The feds had done their research and had learned that Jim and Keith were partners. They also knew that Keith had just been released to the halfway house. They were just wondering who the guy was that was in the car with Keith. Keith flew through traffic with Ramona trying to keep up with him. Fred was use to riding in old school cars. He wasn't use to riding in high end cars. Riding in that Benz at the speed that Keith was driving at, had Fred feeling like he was riding in a space ship.

Fred yearned to get him one. Keith stopped at a couple of spots where he still had niggas working for him. He jumped out of the car to holla at them. Some of them still owed him money, and handed him big knots of money. The feds had followed behind Ramona. They parked a little ways down from where Keith and the men stood talking, but with their camera that was equipped with a zoom in lens, the pictures that they were snapping would come out clear.

After talking to the men, Keith headed back to the shop with Ramona following him and the feds following her. When he got back to the shop, Keith told Jim to hook him and Fred up with some pay stubs. He also told him that he was going to need him to hook them up with some pay stubs, and cover for them if the halfway house contacted him to verify that they would be working there. Jim told him that he would take care of everything.

Keith and Fred jumped back into the car with Ramona and she drove them back to the corner that she had picked them up from. The feds trailed Fred and Keith all the way back to the halfway house. Now they knew that it would not be hard to find out who the guy was that was with Keith.

Chapter 35

Spud realized how dangerous the game that she was playing was, when she saw on the news how four Jamaicans were killed down the street from Spank's stash house. After not seeing Earn for over a week she knew that he had to be one of the dead men. He had not come to retrieve any of his things, including his dope and money.

She drove past the stash house a number of times, but never saw any sign of activity.

After receiving Allen's threat from Dame, she called him. He wanted to meet up with her face to face. She knew that Allen was dangerous. He had almost killed Nanky when he woke up one night and caught her trying to rob him. She knew that he was not gullible like Dame. She met up with him at the BW3 sports bar. He grilled her about everything that she had told Dame.

She stuck to her guns, giving him the same story that she had given Dame. She knew that she had to be careful not to implicate herself.

"So you know nothing about Spank planning to run up in my house or Coco's shop?" Allen asked her.

"Look Allen, I let Spank's crew lay at my house for a couple of weeks, when they first came up here. After two weeks Spank had me rent him a house around the corner from mine. After that I rarely saw Spank. He would come through, every now and then to fuck, but we never had any real conversations."

"So you don't know where the nigga is at?"

"He and one of the Jamaicans that he brought up here with him fell out. The Jamaican joined up with some other Jamaicans from up at Dailey's. Last week four Jamaicans got killed down the street from the stash house. I have been riding by there every day, but ain't nobody been there."

"Spud I am going to be honest with you. If I somehow find out that you had anything to do with what all went on, or that you assisted Spank in any type of way I am going to kill you. Since you seem to know so much about Spank and his crew you have two days to find out where they are at and get back with me."

"Allen I'm trying to help and this is how you are going to play me?"

"Come on Spud, you know that I talked to Dame's hoe ass. You charged that nigga for the information. You ain't trying to help nothing but your pockets. A lot of people have been hurt behind all of this. I noticed that you keep staring at this scar on my face, Spank did this to me. You done got yourself caught up in some serious shit. You a big girl now, you got two days or it's a wrap. You have a good day!" Allen told her as he got up and left.

Spud sat there thinking, "How did I get myself caught up in this shit? Trying to get some get back on Spank, playing games, now my life is on the line." Spud figured that she only had one option, to pack her shit and split town. She headed home to pack her things.

She reached her house, got out of her car and headed up to the door. She put the key into the door and opened it. Before she realized what was happening a hand covered her mouth as a knife appeared at her throat.

"You wicked mon, you devil, me must send you to hell!" A voice said into Spud's ear. The man pushed Spud inside of the house and used the back of his foot to kick the door shut. Spud fearing for her life reached back behind her and grabbed the man's nuts and squeezed hard as she could and the man let out a shriek. The knife went across Spud's neck drawing blood as she broke free and took off running down the hall. The man got his composure and took off running after her. Spud made it to the bedroom and was trying to shut the door when the man bust through it. Spud ran to her bed and reached under her pillow. She felt a sharp pain shoot through her shoulder. She kicked the man and he stumbled back giving her enough time to pull the gun from under the pillow and turn around. When she turned around the man was coming back towards her with the knife raised high in his hand. Spud started firing the gun. After he was hit by three bullets, the man fell to the floor, but Spud kept shooting him until the gun was empty. She ran to the phone and called 911. She hysterically told the dispatcher that she thinks that she had killed a man that had forced his way into her home and attacked her. She also told the dispatcher that she needed medical assistance.

By the time the paramedics and the police had arrived Spud had loss so much blood that she was drifting in and out of consciousness. The paramedics were loading Spud onto a stretcher, while a police officer was removing the mask from the dead figure.

When the mask was removed, Spud saw that it was Jamaican Kris. Her last thought before she lost consciousness was, "Spank tried to kill me!"

☐

Byron and Larry had put the hood on the map. They had Morris Black popping again. They just needed to find a steady connect, they were getting low on dope again and was tired of only being able to get a half of a key here and there. They needed a connect that could provide them with at least two to three birds a week.

Byron was talking to cook it up Pete, while he was blowing up some dope for them. "Damn Pete this is a dry ass town! Since Cleveland ain't got no straight pipeline it be hard to get a decent size package. The niggas that got the dope don't get enough to serve everybody." Cook it up Pete stopped what he was doing for a minute.

"See everybody thinks that Ole Pete ain't good for nothing but cooking up this stuff. Ole Pete use to be a major player in the game. He just went against the rules of the game and let it bring him down. One thing that Ole Pete still got is connections in the game, you boys need a connect? Ole Pete can get you one."

"Pete we ain't talking no small shit! We are talking birds."

"Shit, ole Pete can get you a flock of birds let me see your phone." Byron handed Pete his phone. Pete dialed a number, someone answered and he started talking.

"Jim, I need to see you, I got two of my young boys that know how to fix cars real good. They just need somebody to give them some work. Okay we are on our way." Pete hung the phone up and told Byron and Larry, "We got to go over to 105th and St. Clair. Bring your money, Jim don't play no games. He got to see that y'all are serious."

"Oh, we are serious we are taking our guns too!"

"Listen youngins, you about to join the big leagues. You are not about to be dealing with no little hood niggas. Jim is the real deal you can't walk up in his spot with no guns. You can leave them in the car, but you cannot disrespect the man like that. When you are trying to establish a relationship it is all about trust. Just bring enough money for one bird. See how that goes, and then we can take it from there." Byron and Larry really liked Pete. For a guy that smoked dope he possessed a lot of knowledge and common sense.

"Okay Pete we will do that." Larry said.

"How much does he sell a bird for?" Byron asked Pete.

"Usually it's twenty eight, but I am going to try to get it for y'all for twenty six."

"We are still going to take twenty eight just in case." They grabbed the money, went outside and jumped into Byron's car, then headed towards St. Clair.

Pete directed Byron to an auto repair shop. They got out of the car and entered the shop. They went to the back of the shop, where Pete knocked on an office door.

"Come in!" replied a voice from behind the door, Pete opened the door and stepped into the office with Byron and Larry right behind him. Inside of the room were Jim and two other men. Jim stood up and shook Pete's hand, "Ole Pete, you're still around huh?"

"Yeah, Ole Pete ain't ready to lay it down just yet. I still got some living to do."

"I hear that, are these the two boys that you were talking about?"

"Yeah this is Byron and that is Larry, they are from Morris Black. They are doing the damn thing. They got money, but ain't got nobody to spend it with."

Fred looked at the two boys. He remembered them before he had gone to jail, they had nothing. Now here it was 18 months later and they were looking for a major connect. Fred knew that he had a lot of catching up to do.

"So what are you boys talking about?" Jim asked them.

"We only brought enough to get one for now, but we would like to be able to get at least two or three at a time every week." Keith spoke up, "That sounds cool, but within the next couple of weeks, y'all will start dealing with my man Fred right here. He is from up in y'all area. He will take care of y'all to keep you from having to take a long trip across town." Byron looked at Fred and knew that he looked familiar.

"Didn't you use to have a blue old school Cutlass on 24's?" Fred beamed with pride. "Yeah that was me."

"Okay, let's do this then!" said Byron pulling out the money. Pete spoke up. "Jim, I told them that you would let them get the first one for 26, being as I'm still a couple stacks with you." Jim laughed and said, "One thing about you Pete, you may have lost a lot of things, but you sure haven't lost your memory." Jim got up and left out of the office.

He went out into the shop, walked over to a car and went into its trunk, slid back a secret compartment and pulled out a wrapped up brick of coke. He took the brick back into the office and they made the transaction.

The feds were sitting across the street in a black van. They were happy that their three months of work and sitting in that hot ass van had paid off. They been had Jim's phone tapped and the shop bugged for three months. They had just been waiting to get a major break. Now they had gotten it. They radioed in for back up. They asked for help from the Cleveland PD also.

They had just gotten the whole transaction on tape and they were going to pull the car over to get the evidence. Byron, Larry and Pete got back into Byron's car and pulled off. When they were two blocks away at a red light, they found themselves being surrounded by police cars. "Shit!" Byron said realizing that there was no place to run and that they had no chance of getting rid of the dope or the guns that they had in the trunk. They were all arrested.

Back at the shop a team of DEA agents ran up in it, some of the agents had dogs that alerted them to three different cars as having narcotics inside of them. The police tore the cars apart finding dope inside of stash spots inside of each car. They found fifteen kilos of cocaine all together. Fred and Keith never made it out of the halfway house, before they were taken into federal custody. They were facing a drug conspiracy charge. They both had prior drug arrest, and were about to be faced with a hell of a challenge.

Chapter 36

Coco was sitting up in the hospital room with Tink, when all of a sudden Tink's body started to convulse. The machine that he was attached to started beeping rapidly. Coco screamed out, "Help! Help!" A nurse rushed in to the room and saw what was taking place she rushed over and hit the panic button, while trying to figure out what was wrong with Tink.

A team of nurses and doctors rushed into the room, and one of the nurses escorted Coco out of the room. The doctors realized that Tink was going through cardiac arrest. He was having a heart attack. They tried to stable him, but he flat lined. They tried desperately to use electric shock to restart his heart, but nothing that they tried worked.

At 6:15PM the doctors pronounced Tink dead. They informed Coco and she went ballistic. She started having a panic attack. They had to inject her with a sedative to calm her down. They decided to keep her for a 24-hour observation. She was given a bed on the psychiatric ward.

On the fifth floor of the same hospital, two detectives entered Spud's room. Spud was sitting up watching television, when they entered.

"Hello Ms. Clayton, I am detective Martin and this is my partner detective Sanchez. We are here to ask you a few questions concerning the incident that took place at your home, as well as another incident that took place at a house that has been leased in your name. First let's start with the man that attacked you. Do you know him?"

"No, I do not,"

"Do you have any clue as to why he attacked you?"

"No, I do not,"

"Ms. Clayton, you have a place leased to you, on E. 82nd. A Shooting occurred there last week. Four men of Jamaican descent were killed. During our investigation, we found that the house which was leased to you had been riddled by bullets. Upon further inspection of the inside of the house, it led us to determine that several individuals made a fast exit. Questioning of the neighbors informed us that several individuals had been staying in that house for the last couple of months. They also informed us that there was excessive traffic to and from that house at all hours of the night, which would indicate drug activity. Now before you tell me no again, really think about the connection that I am about to make for you. Several individuals were living in a house that is leased to you. Four Jamaicans were killed in a shootout with the individuals that were staying in that house. Now a couple of days ago another Jamaican comes to your house and tries to kill you. Now if you are going to sit up here and continue to play games and waste our time, as soon as the doctor signs your release papers I am going to have you transferred straight downtown."

Spud realized that she was in a tight situation. She started to think that she could turn it to her advantage and kill two birds with one stone. Dame, she figured she could deal with. She could possibly even continue to extort him. She realized that Allen and Spank were her biggest threats. She thought that if she could get them out of the way, that she could breathe easy. She told the police that she would cooperate.

She started spinning a web of lies to the police. She implicated Spank and Allen in a host of crimes that had recently occurred. She pinned the murders of the Jamaicans on Spank. She told the police that Spank had brought one of the Jamaicans up to Cleveland from Florida and that they had recently fell out over drug money. She even implicated Spank in Tink's shooting, not knowing that Tink had recently died from his injuries.

She thought about the unsolved murder that she had seen on the news, that happened up in Morris Black and she pinned that on Allen. She even went as far as telling the police that Allen had confessed the murder to her.

"You know you may be required to testify before a grand jury and again at trial if these individuals intend to take that route?" Martin told her.

"I guess that I am willing to do whatever must be done to get all of this over with."

"Ms. Clayton, why do you think that Jamaican was really trying to kill you?"

"I think that Spank realized that I knew too much and decided that it would be better to have me killed."

"For your protection, we are going to put you into hiding until we can get these individuals up off of the streets."

"I don't want to sit up in no damn jail!"

"You won't sit in jail we will put you up in a hotel room."

"I guess I could work with that, can I just stop by my house to pick up a few things?"

"I do not think that it would be wise for us to let you do that. It might not be safe. Just give us a few days to work with this information that you gave us. Hopefully we will be able to get them off of the streets quickly, seeing as we have an advantage because they do not know that we are looking for them." The detectives left the hospital. Sanchez said, "You remember Shamar James don't you?"

"How could I forget, he has to be the luckiest guy on the planet. He beat the murder charge and the drug charge last year. We caught him with two kilos of cocaine and he got off on a technicality."

"Well, we got him dead to right this time, with a live witness." said Sanchez.

"I think that we still got an address listed for him on file."

"This other guy, Allen Turner what do you know about him?"

"Well, he doesn't have any priors, so he definitely knows how to stay under the radar."

"This guy Tink aka Tarvis Jones, we arrested him last year with James. They were partners. Now she is saying that James shot him. We have to look into that." said Sanchez. They headed downtown to the station. Martin decided to look up the addresses on Spank and Allen, while Sanchez checked into the shooting of Tink.

They both found what they were looking for. Martin found addresses for Spank and Allen. Sanchez found out that Tink had indeed been shot, and had just recently died from complications related to the shooting.

"We should have enough on James now to bury him under a jail. Five dead bodies that we can connect him to!" said Sanchez.

"I say this time we secure a search warrant along with the arrest warrant this time. We do not want him getting off on any technicality again."

"We can execute the warrants at the same time. You can lead one team while I lead the other. I say we do it around 6:00am."

"That work for me!" Sanchez said.

Spank did not like keeping guns and drugs where he laid his head. He also knew that the neighborhood, that he lived in was not the type that would let a lot of traffic to and from his house go unnoticed. He paid a fiend to rent him another house close to down the way and moved his crew into it.

He was puzzled that he nor any of the other crew members had not heard anything from Kris in over a week. That was not like Kris to just up and disappear like that. Spank figured that if he had been in jail he would have surely contacted one of them by now.

He left the stash house and headed home. He thought about calling Nena, but felt that he needed some rest. At 5:30am the next morning two teams were preparing to execute search and arrest warrants at Spank and Allen's residence. They set their watches in sync. At exactly 6:00am, both teams began affecting their warrants.

One team kicked in Spank's door and made it to his bedroom before he even had a chance to get up out of his bed. He was cuffed, took downstairs and placed on a couch, while the officers conducted a search. After they concluded their search and found nothing, Spank, was transferred down to headquarters.

The second team forced entry into Allen's house and was met by gunfire, Allen heard his door being kicked in and got flash backs of what happened the last time that he had gotten caught slipping. He jumped up out of his bed and grabbed his forty glock. He told the girl that was lying in his bed to go and hide in the closet. Allen ran out into the hallway and heard footsteps coming up the stairs. Trying to surprise the intruders Allen jumped out and started shooting. By the time he realized that it was the police in whom he was shooting at it was too late, he had committed his self. He did get to hit two swat officers before he was riddled with bullets.

Allen was hit thirty two times, to some that was an overkill. Others would say that's what happens when you fire upon police, showing no respect for authority.

The police conducted a search of the house and found a terrified girl hiding inside of the bedroom closet. The girl was taken in for questioning.

☐

Spank was sitting in an interview room, down at the police headquarters. Detectives Martin and Sanchez entered the room. Martin spoke, "So Mr. James we finally meet again." Spank just looked at him without saying a word.

"You won't weasel yourself out of this one James. We have a witness that ties you to the murders of those four Jamaicans and to your ex-partner Tarvis Jones. Would you like to make a statement concerning these allegations?"

"I ain't got nothing to say to y'all, I would like to call my attorney!"

"Have it your way Mr. James." They took Spank down to booking. He was booked and placed into the county jail.

Chapter 37

Jenkins and Howard were called into the station after it was found out that the suspect that they had linked to the murder in which they were investigating had gotten killed while police were trying to apprehend him. What interested them the most was that their murder victim's girlfriend was found hiding in the suspect's closet after he was killed. They decided that they needed to interview her again.

They went down to the interview room to question her. When they stepped in, she had her head down on the table and looked to be crying.

"Ms. Parker." She lifted her head up off of the table and wiped the tears away from her eyes. She remembered the two detectives that stood before her. They had interviewed her the night that Rick was killed.

"Ms. Parker, you know why we are back don't you? This appears to be a strange scenario."

"What are you talking about?"

"Here it is we get a tip that Mr. Turner had killed your boyfriend Mr. Spencer and when the officers execute a search warrant at Turner's house, they find you hiding inside of his bedroom closet. You know how that looks don't you?"

"No! What does it look like?"

"It looks like Mr. Turner was the one that killed your boyfriend and you were the one that set it up."

"That's bullshit! Allen did not kill Rick and I did not set it up."

"How do you know that Turner did not kill Spencer?"

"Because me and Allen were out together that night that Rick got killed."

"You sure that y'all were not out killing Mr. Spencer?"

"Fuck no! We ain't kill nobody!"

"Will you be willing to take a lie detector test to prove that?"

"I'm willing to do whatever it takes to clear me and Allen's name."

"We will have to hold you, until we can set up a reading,"

"Am I under arrest?"

"As of right now technically you are nor under arrest, but we can hold you legally for up to seventy two hours. Hopefully we will have an expert available by then." Cynthia was taken and placed into a holding cell.

□

After Allen was killed and Spank was arrested, Spud was given the okay to return home. Soon as she got home, she called Dame and tried to shake him down for some money. She told Dame that the police was trying to link him to Tink's shooting, and tried to get her to implicate him. She told him that she kept her mouth closed and that she needed that other $10,000 that he promised her so that she could leave town for a while.

Dame told her to meet him at the bus stop up on E. 75th and Kinsman in front of the Arab store. Spud got into her car and drove up to the Arab store. She parked her car in the parking lot, got out and went and stood in front of the bus stop waiting on Dame. While she was waiting a minivan pulled to a stop in front of her. The side door to the van slid open and out jumped two masked men carrying guns. They snatched Spud, jumped back into the van and the van sped off.

Spud's body was found three days later in an empty field. She had been shot in the head twice and set on fire. Martin and Sanchez were notified of her killing. They could not believe it. Every time that they got their hands on James the only witness in the case would come up dead.

"This is crazy! This bastard is going to walk again!" said Sanchez.

"Maybe the streets will eventually deal with him!" said Martin.

"We still have her statement, I'm going to push the DA to pursue a trial based on her statement." said Sanchez.

Martin and Sanchez tried to use Spud's statement to pursue the charges against Spank. Spank's attorney filed a motion with the court, arguing that to make Spank stand trial with only a statement from a dead witness as evidence would violate his sixth amendment right to confront any witness against him.

The judge ruled in Spank's favor, finding that it would be unconstitutional to make Spank stand trial without him being able to confront the witness against him. The charges had to be dismissed the judge ruled.

□

Cynthia passed two lie detector tests, and without anybody to connect her or Allen to Rick's murder, now that Spud was gone they had no reason to hold her anymore and she was released.

Spank was eventually released. He joined back up with his crew. Everything had worked out for him. Tink was dead and Allen was dead.

Spank set out with his crew and took Longwood back over. He met some resistance at first, but after taking out a few people including Ricardo, everyone else started to fall in line. He ruled Longwood with an iron fist, never forgetting how the people down there had turned their backs on him.

Nena became his girl, and he moved her in with him.

The loose end that he felt he had was Dame, with all that Spank had accomplished he still did not feel at peace, he still felt no happiness. He wondered what it would take for him to finally be happy. So far revenge had not done it. He thought that maybe if he dealt with Dame and got some closure then maybe he would feel complete.

He decided to walk through Longwood up to the plaza to get his self something to eat from the Muslim restaurant. He went into the restaurant and ordered something to eat. After his food was ready, he took it and stepped outside of the restaurant. A van pulled to a stop in front of him. The side door slid open, and out jumped two masked men with guns. They ran up on Spank with their guns drawn. One of the men hit Spank repeatedly on the top of his head with a gun, before they finally dragged him into the van and sped off.

This was the second time that people in the plaza had watched a van pull up and snatch someone. They saw Ricardo get returned, they wondered if Spank would have the same luck.

New Flavor Books & Publishing LLC

Book Order form

Full Name: _____

Institution# (If applicable):_____

Address: _____

Address 2: _____

City:_____ State:_____ Zip:_____

Book Title:	Price/Quantity
Hood to Hood: A Cleveland Story	*$15.99* _____
Hood to Hood 2: Spank's Revenge	*$15.99* _____
Sexual Addiction: Director's Cut	*$15.99* _____
All Flavors: A book of Erotic Short Stories	*$9.99* _____
Bisexual Bliss	*$15.99* _____
Murder or Justice	*$15.99* _____
Hittin' Licks	*$15.99* _____

Total Including ($3.00) Shipping and Handling _____

To place an order for one of our books please send a payment
for the price of the book plus $3.00 for shipping and handling to:

New Flavor Books & Publishing LLC

C/O Book orders

P.O. Box 603323

Cleveland, Ohio 44103

Please allow 2 - 4 weeks